Marc drew closer. "Are you afraid of me?" His voice was a sensuous whisper.

"Don't make me laugh."

"Then why are you going so slow?" More of the silky tone. "Rip my shirt off just like the movies."

She focused on the job or risked losing herself in his allure. "I can't afford to buy you another."

"I've got plenty. Come on. Rip it off. I work out. Me Tarzan. You Jane. Rip."

"This is not the jungle." She undid another button.

His eyes narrowed but glinted with slyness. "You *are* afraid of me."

Katrina yanked his shirt apart, buttons flying everywhere. "Satisfied?"

The shirt stuck over his rippled shoulder muscles. "You haven't finished."

She dragged it off, ripped it in half, and threw both pieces in his face. "Ripped."

Laughing, he batted them away.

Hands on her hips, she said. "Any requests for the pants?"

His eyes lit. "With your teeth."

She turned. He pulled her back. "Just joking."

She undid his buckle and pulled his belt off.

Marc drew closer, his lips touching hers. "Unless you're up for it."

The Hockey Player and the Angel

by

Kirsten Paul

Calendar Men of King Court, Book 1

The Hockey Player and the Angel

Cover Art by *Debbie Taylor*

The Wild Rose Press, Inc.
PO Box 708
Adams Basin, NY 14410-0708
Visit us at www.thewildrosepress.com

Publishing History
First Champagne Rose Edition, 2019
Print ISBN 978-1-5092-2645-0
Digital ISBN 978-1-5092-2646-7

Calendar Men of King Court, Book 1
Published in the United States of America

Dedication

To Paul, Anthony, and Christina.

Chapter One

Katrina felt like the howling blizzard outside. Dark, cold, and utterly miserable. The same as when that idiot, who-can't-be-named, left her after discovering she wasn't as rich as he thought. Correction. Since her family put the inn and restaurant up for sale.

Unfortunately, it wasn't toastier inside either. Her three younger sisters hurled darts at her with their ice-blue glares. She expected them to unfurl verbal barbs soon.

"You did what?" Sister number two, Ingrid, her hands on her hips, highlighting her judo-sleek waistline said. If Katrina were as challenging and "in your face" as Ingrid, she wouldn't be in the line of fire but the one firing.

"I said no." Katrina dumped the pail of water in the janitor's sink.

"It's King Court Development's third offer on the inn and property," Ingrid said. "A phenomenal one. It will pay off all the creditors with enough left over to settle Mom and Dad in Florida or wherever they want to retire."

"And, to quote you, for the rest of us to live happily ever after," sister number three, Rebeka, who held the box containing her new designer boots against her chest, said. Leave it to buxom and brainy Rebeka to remind Katrina of every word she uttered—and what she didn't want to remember.

"To live *mildly* comfortably," Katrina replied, closing the maintenance closet door.

"Very soon, we will have to declare bankruptcy," sister number four, Annelise, chimed in, sitting at the table of the restaurant-sized kitchen, downloading music on her cell. Sweet and ingénue Annelise with the angelic smile, who got all the good-natured and happy genes Katrina didn't.

Katrina put her hands on her waist and stared them down in executive sister style. "How can I sell with Dad in the hospital? The massive heart attack six months ago forced him to put the inn and property on the market. I know he jokes about starting a new career or going back to school, but selling will devastate him—and Mom, too."

"And bankruptcy won't?" Ingrid's voice was a whisper, but sharper than any of Katrina's high-end knives.

Katrina brushed past Ingrid and behind the counter to the sinks where the pots and plates from dinner waited to be washed and sterilized. By her. Her sisters weren't interested in anything related to the inn, including cleaning their own plates. "It won't go that far. I told King Court Development I would sell only if the CEO came and saw the inn and property first."

Rebeka moved to the counter, separating Katrina from them. "You still want to sell him on your idea of building ski lifts and golf courses and all the other wonderful and uber-expensive stuff you talk about?"

"It's worth a try, isn't it?" Katrina picked up a pot. "I want a win-win situation. A win for King Court Development and a win for Dad and Mom and for us."

"You mean a win for Dad and Mom and for *you*." Ingrid moved next to Rebeka. "The inn has been in the family for over a hundred and fifty years. It will be a big loss for them. Quite honestly, I think Dad's waiting for it to be sold. Then he can heal and move on with his life. But the restaurant has been in your hands since you graduated from culinary school. You're going to lose your restaurant."

"Fine, it means a big win for me, if I can sway Mr. CEO to my ideas. What's wrong with wanting the restaurant to survive again? It kept us afloat for a long time." Until she shut it down because no one came to the inn or restaurant.

Katrina turned and filled the sink with hot water. She had worked hard to turn a good restaurant into an exceptional one and make her dream come true. But when the inn started losing money, so did the restaurant until she had no choice but to close it down. Now she only opened it for special occasions and those were few and far between. Catering brought in some money but only enough to cover the bills for the family's quarters. Soon she'd have to give catering up, too. It made no money.

Why did her sisters blame her for wanting to bring life back to the only thing she wanted? They merrily moved on beyond the inn. She had nowhere to go. She had nothing else. The Acadia Restaurant and Inn were her life and future. She was nothing without them. A big fat zero.

"You should never have proposed remodeling the inn or restaurant," Ingrid said.

Darts now sprang into Katrina's eyes, as they always did when her sisters blamed her. "Did I know

Mom and Dad would take the renovations so far? Did I know it would ruin us? I can't change what happened." She turned the water off, almost pulling the faucet out. She couldn't confess she beat herself up every day thinking about what happened. She knew she shouldn't have made suggestions, but it was too late now. The inn and restaurant had unraveled past any hope to save them. Only her pride remained, and she'd hold onto it as long as possible—if she could persuade the CEO of King Court Development to her thinking.

"Mom and Dad put the responsibility of selling on me. They even gave me legal authority. What harm is there in asking for a face-to-face meeting?"

Her sisters didn't say anything. They didn't even bat an ice-cold eye. Katrina took it as a sign to continue. "What harm is there in showing the CEO of King Court Development what he'll destroy to build his vast housing empire of cookie-cutter homes? If he still says no, then I sign *before* we declare bankruptcy. End of story."

Katrina turned to the sink and washed the pot. And end of all her hard work and dreams. She would be a verifiable failure.

****

Marc loved making money, the more of it the merrier, but not in a blizzard, and not when his Range Rover shook like a miniature replica car.

"So, remind me why we've put our lives in your hands, Marc?" Jakob asked, leaning forward from the back seat.

"Because you're the rookie still driving his grandmother's station wagon, and I'm the veteran with the expensive Range Rover. I know what I'm doing."

"You mean you're older and wiser?" Jakob asked, with a sly smile.

"I'm richer." He smirked as oohs and aahs and retorts came from all three of his colleagues in the car.

"It's a reason but not a good one, *mon capitaine*," Eric replied. He pressed his hand against the dashboard and peered through the sleet of snow, banging the car without mercy. For a big man, the biggest on the team standing six feet, five inches Eric looked like a frightened boy.

The wipers dragged across the windshield and screeched from the ice. "How about the chance to be rich, too, and make millions of dollars," Marc said, throwing his gloves off to grip the wheel better. "By doing nothing but investing? Housing is in big demand around here. People want affordable and comfortable homes within driving distance of the nation's capital and I, the CEO of the newly-formed King Court Development, along with you three inept business wannabes, and the community of King Court will offer people that opportunity."

Tyler pulled Jakob away from the gap between the seats. He stuck his head through. "If someone told me we'd have to go through winter hell to even get a chance at those millions, I'd say wait for spring. We don't get weather this bad in Detroit."

"Can't remember Stockholm blizzards this bad, either," Jakob said.

Eric grimaced. "Quebec's were comparable. So, we skied, skated, and made babies."

"It will all be worth the trip through this snow chaos," Marc said. He was born and raised in the northern Ontario community of King Court, but the dark, narrow, and winding road didn't have lights. The last time he maneuvered a car through this kind of weather was fifteen years ago before leaving King Court. He came home every summer. In balmy June he visited and was photographed as Mr. January Hockey Player for the "Men of King Court" calendar.

The car swerved.

"Whoa!" his teammates exclaimed as Marc kept his grip on the car.

"Any one regretting not going to the Bahamas, like me?" Eric asked.

"You won't when the contract is signed, giving us the opportunity to make those wonderful millions of dollars." Marc lifted his foot off the pedal and steered the car back onto the road. The car had top of the line four-wheel-drive traction, but the roads were slicker and icier the farther he drove down the isolated road to the Acadia Inn. Turning back wasn't an option. Ottawa was a good half hour away in favorable weather conditions. Montreal, where they started, was another hour and a half away.

The Acadia Inn couldn't be much farther. He'd speak to Katrina Sherrer, the owner of the inn and wait the storm out there. He didn't have any idea what some tête-à-tête with a woman, who was probably as ancient as her inn, would accomplish.

His teammates and he took off several days during the NHL's all-star break. Now, however, he wished he was in the Bahamas like them.

Eric leaned forward. "I think there's a sign coming up." They passed it, but it was blanketed with snow and glazed with ice. "Bahamas, other direction."

****

Katrina was exhausted. She'd been up since five, preparing a luncheon for a curling championship team, and it was after dinner now. But more duties awaited before she fell into her bed and tried not to think about her father in the hospital and the desperate state of the inn. Time to put on the caretaker's hat and make sure everything was tied down outside. She didn't need more damage and expenses from snow, ice, or wind to the old building and vast property.

She threw on her parka, gloves, and hat, draped a scarf around her neck to cover her mouth, and pulled on her hiking boots, tucking her yoga pants inside. Feeling like a child in a bulky snowsuit, she opened the heavy wooden front doors. A blast of wind and snow slammed her against the frame.

"Thank you, god of blizzards, for the refreshing slap." It's just what she needed to keep her awake and alert. She stepped out and wished she could go back inside and snuggle in her bedroom like her sisters. The blizzard could sweep the inn away like a tornado for all they cared. Their extensive wardrobes were safely in their apartments in Toronto or Ottawa. They only brought the minimal for their holiday stay with her parents.

Why couldn't she be more like her sisters? More uncaring? "I hate me," Katrina mumbled as she threw her hood over her head, tightened the strings, and pushed herself through the elements. She was the oldest but since the inn went under, she accepted hand-me-downs—or rather hand-me-ups—from her sisters.

She held onto the wooden railing and walked down the short flight of steps, sinking into ankle deep snow. It whipped against walls and edges. That was good. It meant less shoveling and plowing for her when the storm ended.

But it could change. The blizzard seemed temperamental.

Keeping her hood over her eyes, she made it to the drive. She caught hold of a lamppost as she slid. Black ice, the worst possible winter condition. No one could tell the difference between black pavement and black ice. She hoped her mother hadn't left the hospital and was stuck on the road. She'd call her when she got back inside and make sure she stayed overnight with her aunt.

With her head down and her back to the wind, she half slid, half ambled across the driveway. Her father kept a barrel of salt and sand at the parking lot entrance just for these icy occasions. She made it when a strong gust of wind whipped her around like a cloth doll. She held onto the barrel for support as ice pelted her face. Keeping one hand on her hood and over her eyes, she tried to lift the lid, but the wind made it difficult to pry open.

This was ridiculous. The wind would just carry the salt away. It was time to get inside—and worry about the driveway in the morning when the storm subsided.

Fighting the sleet, she moved toward the house then stopped and listened. Was that a car? She wasn't expecting guests, and she didn't think any of her sisters' friends were foolish enough to drop in during a blizzard.

Lights pierced through the night and snow intermittently, like a lighthouse's faint beams in a blanket of fog. If it was a car, then it was having difficulty maneuvering on the black ice.

She took a few steps toward the inn when a big SUV emerged out of the dark sleet like an animal leaping onto its prey. Screaming, she ran but slid and fell. The car swerved, skimming her and smashed into the stone wall beside the parking lot. A deafening boom and the crush of steel silenced the wind and froze her to the spot.

Chapter Two

Ice hit her face and wind flipped her hood off. Was she still alive? Holy shit. She was. Just narrowly. The car could have thrown her to the veranda.

Her pulse racing, Katrina bolted up. The bumper was mangled, and the hood crumpled up in a V. Smoke billowed out of the engine.

She didn't know how, but she rushed to it. Four men were trapped inside. The air bags had deployed but no one was moving.

Were they dead? Had she killed them when they swerved to avoid her?

She pulled at a door, but it was locked. "Open the doors!" *Please, God, let them be alive.*

Nothing.

She raced to the driver's window and banged. "Open the doors. Please, open the doors." *And please be alive.* She couldn't have the accident of these four men on her conscience on top of the inn and restaurant.

The locks clicked open. Katrina sighed in relief. Someone was alive. She yanked the driver's door open. All were big and strong-looking men in heavy parkas or wool overcoats.

"Please all be alive," she shouted. "Please tell me you're okay."

No one answered. But someone clicked the doors open. Did he click with his dying breath? Maybe they were in shock. Please let them be alive. What could she do? How would ambulances get here if they were hurt? She was doomed.

Three of the men moved their heads against the airbags.

She breathed in relief. "Three out of four. Good. You're alive." Now for the driver. His head remained on the airbag as it deflated. "Please be alive, too." Her hand shaking, she placed her finger on his neck. He was warm and had a strong pulse. "Four out of four." She looked to the sky. She didn't care if ice scratched her face. "Thank you, God. Thank you." She put her hand on his arm. "Can you hear me, sweetie?"

The driver slightly moved his head. "Sweetie?"

Katrina wanted to cry in joy.

"*Sweetie* is my dad," he murmured, "when he's in trouble."

"You're not in trouble." But she would be when they learned who caused their accident.

Katrina watched the driver as he moved his head back against the seat and grimaced. Blood oozed from his nose. He opened his eyes, but they only fluttered. "Can you check…the others…*honey*?"

Katrina didn't know whether to laugh or to cry. "*Honey* is my mother—when my dad's in trouble."

The man behind the driver pulled himself against the seat and pressed the air out the deployed bag. "I'm okay. *Sweetie and honey.*"

Katrina wanted to sing out her praises.

"I'm fine, too, thank you," said the man beside him, pushing back his shoulder-length blond hair from his forehead. "Eric?" He gripped the passenger seat and pulled himself forward. "Check Eric." He indicated the man in front.

Katrina dashed to the passenger side, half sliding and half running. She pulled on the partially opened door, but it was jammed. The blond in the back seat kicked open his door. He got out but slid to the ground. Katrina grabbed him. He was taller and bigger than she thought and almost fell with him.

"You're not in any condition to help." Katrina settled him against the car. "You're hurt."

"No, I'm okay. Really. I feel worse when I'm hit by some two-hundred and thirty-pound defenseman." He grabbed the passenger door and pulled but it wouldn't open.

"Stand back," Eric yelled, surprising both Katrina and the blond.

"You're alive," the blond said.

"Us French-Canadians are invincible. You should know by now, Jakob."

Katrina and Jakob stepped aside. Eric took his seat belt off, turned, and with one big hit, kicked the door open.

"He's one of those two-hundred and thirty-pound defensemen I was talking about."

"And lucky to have me on your team, rookie."

Katrina put her hands on Eric's jaw, turning his face. "You may be invincible, but you look a little— worked in now." He had a few cuts, but he didn't squirm in pain. "How do you feel?"

"A little, well, a little loose." He peered at the driver. "Marc, you okay? Are you foggy?"

Marc's head dropped onto the deflated air bag of the steering wheel.

"Marc?" Eric jostled his shoulder.

Marc sighed dramatically and shook his head. "Can't…a guy get a-a-any rest around…here?" His words were slurred.

"You foggy, Marc?"

"*I'm* invincible, Eric." He pulled his head back against the seat. "Now get out of my car." The slurring was gone.

"I need to get all you invincible lot inside," Katrina said. "Marc—*sweetie*, can you honk the horn for me? I need help from my sisters inside."

Marc turned his head, but his eyes remained closed. Blood flowed over one of his eyes from his eyebrow. But he didn't say anything, frightening Katrina.

"Marc?" she shouted.

"Yes, honk. I heard, *honey*." His hand moved to the steering wheel, but he took a long moment to locate the horn. The screech filled the air, making the men cringe. Eric noticed and glanced at Jakob. It was obvious to everyone. Marc was disoriented.

"Don't stop honking, Marc, okay?" Katrina said. It would keep him alert until she got him out. "Let's get you inside, Eric. Can you stand up?"

"No problem." He swung his feet over the side and gripped the door and car. He pulled himself up only to slide. Katrina grabbed him and was thankful Jakob did, too. Eric was as big as a heavy-weight wrestler. He draped one hand around her shoulder and the other around Jakob and together they moved toward the inn.

On the veranda, she flung open the front doors and carried him into the lobby to a wing chair, dropping him there. Jakob slumped into an opposite wing chair.

"Annelise, Rebeka, Ingrid," Katrina shouted. "Get

here, now."

Jakob sprung up. "We should go out and help the others."

"No, Jakob, you stay put and make sure Eric is okay. My sisters should be here any minute. I'll help the others."

She raced back outside, fighting the wind and snow and sleet. The man in the back seat stepped out and leaned against the side. The car horn blared on and off.

"I think I hurt my foot," the man said.

"We'll get you inside and take a look." She peered into the driver's side, put her hand over Marc's, and pulled it off the horn. "You're doing a good job, Marc. I'm bringing another of your invincible buddies inside and then come right back for you. You hang in there, okay?" She waited, but there was no response. "Marc, can you hear me?"

"Has anyone ever told you you're bossy, *honey*?"

Katrina managed a wry smile. "Many times, *sweetie.*"

"I'll hang in there. I promise."

She pushed his hand over the horn again. "Keep honking." It was the only way to keep him alert—and her satisfied.

She helped the man in the dark parka maneuver the ice. He couldn't put his left foot down, but he tried. She got him inside the inn and into another wing chair around the coffee table. Jakob took off his coat and helped Eric.

"I think Eric's okay," Jakob said. "I don't feel any broken bones." He turned to the other young man. "Tyler, you okay, buddy?"

"My foot is sore, but I think I can walk it off."

14

Katrina headed toward the front door again. Where the hell were her sisters? They probably had their earbuds on as they usually did, blotting out the world around them and especially her. "Ingrid! Rebeka! Annelise!" she shouted, startling the men. "My sisters," she told them in explanation.

"Hope they're evil," Eric said.

"You may get your wish," Katrina said and rushed out again, keeping her back to the wind as she made her way to Marc. The car horn stopped blaring. Fear filled her again. She hurried to the car. Marc lifted his head and rested it against the seat. Blood smeared his face. Other than his nose and eyebrow, she couldn't tell from where else it came.

"The honking was bothering me," Marc said.

"Not a problem. It's your turn now." She pulled off her scarf and wiped the blood from around his eye, so he could see.

The man's eyes flickered opened. Light blue eyes took her in as she dabbed at the blood around his nose.

"You're an angel, *honey*. Bossy but an angel."

"If I were an angel, *sweetie*, I would have used my wings to get out the way. Then you wouldn't have crashed to avoid me."

He smiled, and it was so warm she forgot she stood in a blizzard. "You're still an angel."

"And you're a sweet talker."

He chuckled. "I'm a sweetie, remember?"

"And invincible."

"Of course." Katrina hoped he was, but the blood on his face proclaimed him a mortal with very warm eyes and a sly smile that made her blush like a school girl.

The dashboard butted against his legs. She bent down and helped him maneuver his feet out. Once they were on the ground, he draped his arm around her shoulders, and pulled himself out. Katrina was a tall woman but slight in built. Marc was as big as his friends. Maybe it was adrenaline or fear, but she didn't know how she was managing to get these men inside.

Carefully, they moved toward the inn. Ice pelted at her as much as it did at Marc. He dragged his hand up to protect her face and used his body to shield her.

Katrina was taken aback. Was he protecting her? She couldn't remember the last time someone protected her. She was the one protecting everyone—her parents, her sisters, and now the inn. It was unexpected and nice. More than nice. It made her want to cry.

But sentimentality wouldn't bring Marc inside. Hard work would. She flung self-pity aside and moved into the lobby. Jakob and Eric rushed toward her, took Marc, and brought him to the sofa. Katrina closed the door, shutting off the screeching blizzard, and threw off her hat and gloves.

Where the hell were her sisters? She was about to pull out her cell phone when Rebeka, Ingrid, and Annelise rushed into the lobby from the kitchen. They stopped short at the sight of the four men.

"I knew Santa Claus was going to be late this year," Annelise exclaimed.

Chapter Three

Katrina normally never agreed with her sisters, but this time, she did. The men were better than good-looking and far more physically fit and shaped than their average counterparts. They had the kind of well-chiseled bodies Katrina only saw on athletes. They all were well-dressed too in suits and shoes she was certain came from designer shops and cost a couple grand.

She couldn't keep her gaze off Marc. He seemed disoriented in the car but now he sat composed. He took in the lobby, his gaze roaming from the oak bar displaying the one-of-a-kind wines and liqueurs, to the huge wood-burning fireplace, to the carved oak doors leading to the restaurant, and all the nineteenth century furniture as casually as he dabbed at the blood dripping from his nose. But she couldn't tell if he approved or not. Whatever he thought, with his arms stretched over the top of the sofa, he owned it as well as everything else in the lobby.

She recognized the long, unwavering, and unemotional look all too well. It was the mark of someone who held power, was rarely challenged, and almost always won—like all the executive chefs she knew. They barked out orders, demanded nothing short of excellence, and didn't appreciate input. But none of the executive chefs she worked for ever made her feel uncomfortable or vulnerable. She was up for any of their jobs or demands. Heck, she was on her way to being one of them. Except for this gorgeous non-chef sitting in front of her, who probably didn't know the difference between a russet potato and a King Edward potato and made her believe it wasn't important, either.

She lifted her hand to her hair. Thank goodness the band she tied around it this morning kept her curls at bay. But she was sure she looked a disheveled mess.

She pulled off her boots and shoved her feet into her sneakers. This unease wasn't good. She had to deal with him—and his colleagues.

But he looked familiar. She was sure he had never been to the inn or the restaurant. She would not forget those discriminating eyes as they ordered the uber-expensive filet mignon with whatever type of potato she offered. Or the well-sculptured body as it jogged around the property without breaking into a sweat. Or the I-am-the-king of whatever seat and room I occupy—and you are my servant. Whether he looked familiar or not, she couldn't gawk—and neither could her sisters. They had seen men before. All kinds of men. Short, tall, stout, muscular, blond, ginger, and so much more.

Just none like these men and certainly no one who made her forget herself like Marc. Maybe the god of blizzards sent them to make the snowstorm bearable. Or maybe she was just man-starved and overworked and wanted to believe Santa Claus hadn't forgotten her and sent her this man as a belated Christmas present. Maybe the god of jackpots would also send funds to save the inn from bankruptcy.

Katrina coughed, hoping to clear her thoughts and get herself moving. She didn't believe in gods, and

Santa Claus forgot about her a long time ago.

"They're not belated Christmas presents, ladies. They're gentlemen who need our help. Their car smashed into the parking lot wall." She didn't tell them it was her fault. The scolding and mocking would be endless. Unless, of course, they high-fived her for dragging in a jackpot of men. "Now get over here and help me. I have no idea how hurt they are."

Her sisters zoomed around the front desk with the biggest smiles, almost tripping over each other.

"Should I call 911?" Annelise asked, taking out her cell. But she stopped short when her gaze fell on Jakob, removing his jacket to reveal a solid and firm chest pressing against a deep blue suit and crimson tie. If this were a movie, the sound of hearts thumping, violins playing, and Cupid shooting arrows into both of them would be heard and seen.

Jakob's face turned red with a boyish smile. "Hey."

Annelise, the youngest but the tallest of them, and her ever-present smile all but floated to him. "Hey."

He held out his hand. "I'm Jakob."

She took it, but they didn't shake. "Annelise." Still no handshake. "Are you hurt, Jakob?"

"Not a bit." He pulled back his broad shoulders, standing a good head over her baby sister. "Just groggy."

"The kid can't score on ice, but he just scored big now," Tyler said, taking off his jacket.

Ingrid slid up to Tyler. Tall with a body that exercised religiously and didn't ingest anything but organic food, except the sweets Katrina baked, Ingrid was a force to reckon with. "Can you score?" She took his jacket.

Tyler smoothed out his dark hair. "Leading scorer on the team and league, until I fractured my finger last month." He held up his right index finger with the splint.

"And off the team and league?" Ingrid was so confident. She also had a high-level black belt in judo. If Tyler or any other man tried anything she didn't like, he felt the repercussions. That's why her second oldest sister did well as a lawyer in a corporate law office on Bay Street in Toronto, and why she wasn't afraid to say what she wanted and to whomever.

"Can't complain," Tyler said. "But I've been in a little drought—until now—maybe?"

"You have any complaints about your body, Leading Scorer?"

Katrina watched Ingrid ease herself closer to Tyler. Tyler answered and moved in too. Lust ricocheted off each other's bodies. He was Ingrid's type. Fearless as well as a player. Katrina shook her head in dismay. He was a guest, not a pickup at a club.

"The name's Tyler."

She extended her hand. "Ingrid."

He kissed it. "Maybe you can check for bruises and help me walk off whatever is ailing my foot, Ingrid."

She dropped his jacket on the coffee table. "My pleasure. Where should I look for bruises?"

Katrina picked up the jacket and handed it to Ingrid. "You can start by hanging Tyler's nice jacket on the antique stand called a coat hanger by the front desk and turning down the X-rated tones. Then a couple questions should help you zero in on any cuts or bruises. The lobby should be big enough for you to graciously help Tyler walk off any lingering pain."

Katrina heard Marc chuckle but avoided staring him down. He was amused by her demands, but she was a professional and got things done.

She tried not to glance and drool over him.

Eric sat up and stared at Rebeka as though he had never seen a woman before. Even with her golden-blonde hair tied back and her eyes hidden behind glasses, Rebeka was a knock out. She was the only one with ample boobs as she often bragged. Her sisters countered she was the only one with ample hips too, which always upset her. "Eric was in the passenger seat, Rebeka," Katrina said. "He was disoriented."

"I'll take care of him." Rebeka went down on her knees to face him. "You still disoriented, Eric?"

"If you're two, then *qui*. If you're one, then *non*."

"French?"

"French Canadian." He bowed his head and put his hand over his heart as though he were a knight. "Eric Cormier."

Rebeka acknowledged with a prim nod. "*Mon plaisir, Eric. Je suis Rebeka.*"

"You speak French?"

"And German, Spanish, Italian, Klingon, and Dothraki."

Eric's eyes lit up as if on fire. "So do I. *Wirklic, so auch ich. Realmente, yo también. Davvero, così lo faccio io.*" He thumped his chest with a clenched right fist. "*Qapia'. M'athchomaroon.*"

Rebeka moved forward, her eyes wide with surprise. "*Wie wundervoll, qué maravilloso, che meraviglia.*" She thumped her chest with a clenched right fist. "*Maj. Athdavrazar.*"

"Yes, it most certainly is wonderful, isn't it?" Eric

replied.

Katrina shook her head in dismay. Who would have thought? Two intellectuals and science-fiction geeks with common ground. Soon they'd discuss foreign books and upcoming sci-fi movies.

Good. The three men were in innocent, lascivious, or intellectual hands. Capable enough.

She now wished she had another sister, one to take care of Marc. She wasn't in the least faint of heart, but she wasn't sure she could handle him without falling over herself like some star-struck thirteen-year-old.

Not that she would dare do anything silly like make a move on Marc. If her instincts were right about him, he was selective, expecting, and getting nothing short of a Victoria's Secret supermodel. She was just the eldest daughter of a near-bankrupt innkeeper, who once thought herself an up-and-coming three-star chef. And she only wore clearance-item Victoria's Secret bras.

"I guess I'm your belated Christmas present," Marc said. His lips turned up at the corners as though teasing her. He still wore his coat but unbuttoned. A narrow reddish-brown tie highlighted an impeccable charcoal suit.

"You may be wishing one of my sisters was unwrapping you after you've been with me. I don't swoon, slink, or speak any sci-fi language."

His smile was nothing short of James Bond's. "I'm not afraid of being manhandled, especially by a beautiful woman."

"You can cut the sweet-talking, now, *sweetie*." She whipped off her industrial-looking parka and threw it on a chair. Compared to him she felt dowdy in her black yoga pants and work out jacket. "You're out of the cold."

"I wasn't sweet-talking. I never sweet-talk. I don't have to."

Wow. Good looks, athletic body, money, and an ego tying them all together. Her instincts were right. He was in a league she didn't care much for. Like he-that-can't-be-named, her last so-called beau.

"Humble I'm not, my beautiful angel. And neither should you. You brought in four brutes all on your own. We owe you a very big thank you." He extended his hand. "It's Marc. Marc Johansen. Sorry, if I don't get up."

"Marc Johansen?" She extended her hand—and pulled it back, surprising him. "Marc Johansen, the hockey player?" She took in his three friends. "You're all hockey players—with the Montreal team. My father is a big Montreal fan."

"And you? Since you don't know our name, you obviously aren't."

"I've held my father's hand when you lost."

"Ouch, now that hurts."

She extended her hand—and pulled it back, again surprising him. "You're also Mr. January Hockey Player on the King Court Calendar."

Could this—he—get any better—or worse?

"Now I know where I've seen you. Where I've seen a lot of you as a matter of fact. You without your hockey gear on—or anything else."

Marc laughed as her sisters bolted to him. "What? You're kidding? No way." They crowded around her. Even though his nose and eyebrow bled, his smile was sly as much as sexy.

"Holy crap. You are Mr. January," Rebeka said.

"The hockey stick was positioned rather strategically," Ingrid said.

"Held in place very strategically, as a matter of fact." Marc dabbed at the blood around his nose with a cotton handkerchief. "I especially liked where the photographer placed the puck."

Visions of him and the puck and hockey stick danced in Katrina's head—and probably in her sisters' heads.

"You're hanging in the office," Annelise said. "My mother has even seen you," she added in a low voice. "My dad thinks he should have been asked. He would have posed with a hammer and saw."

Marc's smile was sly with no hint of bashfulness. "All proceeds went to charities of our choice. I was more than happy to pose with a strategically placed puck and hockey stick." He pulled the handkerchief away. "No one's thrown any darts at me?" His gaze moved to Katrina. "Including the boss here?"

Katrina didn't show any surprise. Just as she pegged Marc as a certain type, he pegged her a certain type, too. The boss. Well, shallow he wasn't. He wasn't off the mark either. "I don't throw darts. I throw knives."

Marc's eyes rounded but his smile didn't relent. He wasn't in the least intimidated but looked intrigued. "I'll make sure to remember."

"Hey, we're hurting here, ladies," Tyler said.

Her sisters moved back to the men.

"Am I going to be honored with your name, now?" Marc asked. "Or do I keep calling you angel or *honey*?"

"I'm sorry." She extended her hand. "It's Katrina. Katrina Sherrer." Marc's smile evaporated as his hand went limp around hers. Katrina's heart plunged. He *was* in a lot of pain. Great. She was in for a lawsuit. More money she could never pay. "You're not feeling well, are you? You're in pain? You're really dead, right?"

"No, no, I'm fine, believe me. My heart is beating well." He withdrew his hand. "It's my foot. I could use some ice for it."

So could she. But for her head. He had far too much ego for her liking, but she didn't know why she reminded herself. "Yes, of course. I'm sorry. Your face needs to be cleaned again and bandaged this time. Your nice handkerchief is getting soaked." She strode to the front desk, grabbed a box of tissues, and brought it to him. "Can I get you set up in a room first? I don't think you're going anywhere tonight."

He took the box of tissues. "Even if my car were driveable, no, I don't think so." He pulled a smile, but it was weak. There was no more James-Bond flash in it, which made her uneasy. He was hurt more than he let on.

She focused on the others. Eric walked around and showed Rebeka he had shaken off any damage and was well enough to dance. Ingrid massaged Tyler's hand and supposedly fractured finger. Annelise and Jakob sat around an unlit fireplace. They gazed into each other's eyes and laughed at some private joke. "I think I'd better get everyone a room."

"Things could get steamy?" Marc asked.

Katrina felt her face go hot as she moved to the front desk. Yes, she wanted to say. For everyone except her and him.

But all the rooms were cold. She always kept the furnace turned off when there were no guests in the rooms. The lobby had its own furnace as did the kitchen, dining room, restaurant, and the private rooms the family called their quarters and home.

The lights flickered several times. Katrina stiffened as everyone expressed surprise.

This wasn't good. She'd better put the men in rooms with wood-burning fireplaces just in case the power went out. The backup generator was disconnected to cut costs. Only her father knew how to connect it.

What a time to be without her parents. Marc dabbed at the blood around his nose. What a time to feel helpless and attracted.

Okay. One problem at a time. She'd worry about heat if the power went out. She had to worry about Marc now—and the others, of course. But he was the one holding back on the extent of his injuries.

She moved behind the front desk and turned on the thermostat for the guest rooms. She waited, knowing it would take a couple seconds to kick in, but nothing happened.

She reset it and turned it on again.

Nothing still.

Shit. What the hell was wrong with the furnace? One click always got it going.

She tried again. Still nothing.

She poked her head out the door. "Annelise?" She was the future engineer. She had to know how to start it. Annelise smiled prettily at Jakob but did not move. "Could I see you for a moment, please?"

Annelise pulled her "I'm not amused" face. "Excuse me, Jakob." She slipped off the stool and went to the back room.

"The furnace isn't working," Katrina murmured.

"You need to turn on the thermostat."

"No kidding."

"You tried?"

"You try now."

Annelise turned it on but nothing happened. She tried again, still nothing. "I think you may need to go downstairs to the furnace room and start it there. Dad did when it didn't kick in."

The furnace room? Katrina gulped. She hated going down there. Not only did the furnace look like a huge and scary octopus ready to entangle her in one of its arms, but it was in the sub-basement where it was dark and cold and possibly had ghosts or monsters or giant insects. Ever since the first time she went at five years of age, she had never gone again without her father or mother. But neither was here to go with her or support her.

God, did she miss them.

"You go," Katrina said.

Annelise moved back. "Me? I do wires. I don't do machines, let alone furnaces. I wouldn't know what to do. Dad taught you."

"Then come with me."

"I don't go to the basement at night."

"You've got to get over that. We have guests. We can't make them freeze."

"Take Rebeka."

"Rebeka is useless."

"Then Ingrid."

"She's more useless."

"Well, I'm not going."

"Fine." She wished she could send her to her room

without dinner. "I'll do it myself. Just give each of the men a corner room with a fireplace in case I can't get the furnace going."

"Jakob can bunk with me."

"He bunks with you, and I'll have to break his legs."

Annelise rolled her eyes. "Dad's not here, Katrina."

"I'm here, and I follow his rules when he's not around."

"Is this because I don't want to go down to the furnace room?"

"This is because you're not sleeping with a man under my watch in this inn. I respected Dad's rule. Ingrid and Rebeka respected it, and now you will, too."

"Fine, I'll check the furnace—with Jakob."

"You're still not sleeping with him."

She stormed off. "Then I'm not checking any furnace."

Katrina looked to the ceiling. She hoped she didn't have daughters. She'd had her fill with her three sisters who never listened or wanted anything to do with the inn.

Clearing her face of anxiety, she returned to the front desk and grabbed four turnkeys and the matching swipe cards for the corner rooms. She kept one set for Marc and gave one to each of her sisters with instructions to bring the men to a guest room. She went back to the sofa. Marc had taken off his coat and stemmed the bleeding from his nose.

"I'm going to set you up in the closest room with a fireplace just in case we lose power and heat. But the closest room is down the hall."

"Not a problem. One of the guys can help me."

But Jakob was entranced with Annelise, Tyler was showing Ingrid what judo moves he knew, and Eric was deep in a Dothraki or Klingon conversation with Rebeka.

"Doesn't look like any of them know you exist," Katrina said.

Marc pulled himself off the sofa, cringing when his foot touched the ground. "Then it's just you and me, kid."

Yup. Just her and the man who had posed nude with only a strategically-placed puck and hockey stick. She slung her arm around his waist and nestled into his side. Heat ricocheted from his body. She wanted to both run away and snuggle closer. *Be professional, Katrina. Professional.* She gulped. Professional was so hard. "Let's go. *Sweetie.*"

Chapter Four

With his arm slung around her shoulder, Katrina
led a hobbling Marc down the hall to the farthest room.
She was about to swipe the card through the pad of the
solid oak door when Marc put his hand over hers. He
indicated the old-fashion turnkey under the swipe pad.
"Does it work?"

"Sometimes."

"Do you have the key?"

Katrina pulled out the pewter turnkey from her
pocket.

"I don't think I've ever seen one of those keys
except in old movies my great aunt and I used to watch.
Can we try it? I'm curious."

Katrina put it in the keyhole, but it wouldn't turn
let alone unlock the door. "They were supposed to add
to the flavor of antiquity and richness, but guests kept
losing them or they wouldn't turn so my dad went back
to the swipe locks." She tried a second time. Still
nothing. Then a third with the same result. She gave up.
"I'm swiping."

"May I?" He took the turnkey. With one turn, he
opened the door. "It just needs a little tender loving
care."

Like she did.

He handed it to her, but she pushed it back. "Keep
it. You'll need it. It's your room. And this, too." She

gave him the swipe card. "Just in case the turnkey becomes moody."

Marc dropped both in his jacket pocket and shuffled in. "Whoa. The lobby is charming, but this room is stunning. The twenty-first century meets the nineteenth century."

"And the eighteenth century. My ancestors collected everything in here. It's part of what makes the Acadia Inn unique."

He ran his hand over the walnut wash stand close to the door. "Everything looks so new, though. Old but at the same time new." He did a double take at a fair-sized flat-screen TV over the wash stand.

"My father is a carpenter or rather an artist. He repairs and maintains all the furniture and woodwork in the entire inn as did my grandfather and his father."

Marc limped to the bed and held onto one of the tall carved four posters, his gaze landing on the clawed feet. "What kind of wood is this?"

"Everything in here, the bed," she pointed to the far wall, "armoire, dresser, and desk are walnut and from the 1880s or 90s. The pieces around the room are also from about the same time. The painting over the bed is an original painting by one of the few female artists of the late nineteenth century, Marie-Anne Couture. She was a maid here at the inn. My great-grandmother found her paintings in her bedroom after she died and put them up around the inn."

"Do they have any artistic value?"

"Never bothered to find out. They've been at the Acadia Inn so long they're part of the wall." She wanted to add she was sure they had artistic merit, but then she might have to let them go to an art gallery. She couldn't part with them, just like the inn, but he didn't need to know her sad story. It would make her feel lower than scum.

"Fascinating history," Marc said. "Are all the guest rooms like this?"

She moved past the Queen Anne chairs to the fireplace and switched on the light. "Every room has its own look and furniture and an original piece from the 1880s forward—except the bathrooms. We don't want our guests to go outside. But they do have an antique look and charm to them. We had a five-star rating when we were in business."

"Your father couldn't have done all the work by himself."

She went to the night table and switched on a decorated pottery kerosene oil lantern, transformed to a modern-day lamp. The room basked in a warm light. It brought images of snuggling in front of the fireplace with the right man—with Mr. January Hockey Player if she allowed herself to dream about being with Mr. Big Ego here.

"No, he had a team at one time. When my parents made the major renovations to the inn, they contracted out a lot of the work." If only Marc knew how much her parents spent on repairing and maintaining the furniture and making the massive overhauls to the rooms and décor to meld the antique with the convenience of the modern. She hated to look at the ledgers. She cried now when she did.

If only she hadn't suggested the renovations and innovations, then maybe they wouldn't be close to bankruptcy. She wanted to modernize the inn and keep its authenticity, but her parents took it back to its roots.

She still blamed herself. She was studying in Paris at the time and never realized how much her parents planned. They went overboard and would never resurface in their lifetime or hers. She was as much at fault for the demise of the inn and restaurant as her parents—more so since, as her sisters often reminded her, she wanted the changes. She should have stopped the renovations but didn't. That was her second biggest blunder. She believed the overhaul could only help the inn and restaurant. Instead, they worked against them.

Maybe she was the one with the big ego and not Mr. January Hockey Player. She wanted the changes to benefit her and her restaurant.

She cleared her thoughts and throat. "We should take a look at your foot. Let's get you on the bed."

Marc sat on the edge and bent over to take off his shoes. Katrina noticed he gripped the duvet. When he straightened himself, his eyes closed for a long moment.

She didn't like the look. "You hurt your back, didn't you? I think I'd better call an ambulance."

She was about to return to the front desk, but he took her hand. His fingers weaved through hers, turning her to mush. "I'm fine, really. My back is okay. It's my foot. It's throbbing."

Katrina didn't want to loosen her fingers but did. "You need to be checked by a doctor."

"I'll take an angel over a doctor anytime—even if she throws knives."

Mr. Smooth-Talker had a sense of humor. Katrina shook her head to hide a smile. "I'll untie your shoes." She went on her knees and removed his shoes and socks. "What was all that business about being foggy in the car?"

"Just overreaction. I suffered a mild concussion a couple weeks ago. Eric was concerned."

"The crash could have aggravated it. You did hit your head against the airbag."

He shrugged. "We all hit our heads against an airbag. I was a little dizzy out there in the car and just now, but I'll rest and be fine soon."

She stared at him long and hard. Katrina knew concussions in sports weren't good. They had ruined many budding sports careers. Ingrid suffered a concussion during a black belt competition and it took several months to recover. Marc looked like he was in his late twenties or early thirties. He still had a number of years ahead of him in hockey if the concussion was minor and a one-time occurrence.

His eyes narrowed as though he sensed her doubts. "I'm fine, really. I have a team of doctors, coaching staff, and management brass who do enough worrying for me."

"I'm sure they do."

"Once I get back to Montreal, I'll be checked by the team doctors and so will my three comrades out there." He swung his feet onto the bed and fell back into the cushions.

Katrina rolled up the right leg of his pants to his calf. His ankle and foot were slightly swollen. She touched them. "I can't tell if anything's broken."

"I can. Nothing is."

"Not the first time?"

"Not in the least. It's a bruise. It'll be black in the morning and uncomfortable to walk on, but I'm fine."

"I'd better get some ice." She eyed his face and the

streaks of dried blood. "But I'd like to clean your face again. Blood is smeared everywhere." She moved to the bathroom in the farthest corner of the room and returned with a wet hand towel. She sat on the edge of the bed and dabbed his face cleaning the blood off. Marc kept his gaze on her. She pretended not to notice but squirmed. She was not only a disheveled mess but didn't have a stitch of makeup on. She was bare, as though she had no clothes on. Worse, no protection.

Why, oh why, didn't she put on makeup that morning? She always did.

"I won't be stabbing you, don't worry," she said.

Marc chuckled. "Not with a hand towel you won't."

She stood up and examined her handiwork. His nose wasn't bleeding but the cut over his forehead needed some rubbing alcohol and a thick bandage. It could bleed again.

"Presentable?" he asked.

More than presentable. Cuts or no cuts, he was gorgeous. Damn gorgeous.

His forehead started to bleed. She mentally shook herself. This ogling would not do. "I need to get the first aid kit. You're," she touched her eyebrow, "bleeding again."

She rushed out of the room and plied herself against the wall, under one of Marie-Anne Couture's paintings of the fields around the inn in the spring. She took a deep breath of relief. He wasn't humble by any means, but he was surprisingly easy-going and charming. She had to distance herself from him. She'd never get anything done if she spent too much time dreaming about a man who was in a league she didn't want to ever play in again.

She strode to the lobby. Her sisters, Eric, Tyler, and Jakob sat in the armchairs around the fireplace, engrossed in conversation.

"You can't flip me," Tyler said to Ingrid who sat on the arm of his chair.

"Don't dare me, Mr. Leading Scorer."

"Go for it," Eric said. "I'll give you a hundred dollars if you can flip him, Ingrid." He even showed her the bill in his wallet.

Children, Katrina thought. She went into the kitchen and grabbed the first aid kit. She heard a bang and "ohs!" coming from the lobby. She rushed back. Tyler lay on the rug in the middle of the armchairs, staring up at Ingrid. She crossed her arms over her chest in a "told you so" expression, while the others laughed or mocked Tyler.

"My finger is okay." He held up the finger with the splint.

Ingrid tossed her blonde-streaked light hair off her face and turned to Eric with an outstretched hand. "A hundred dollars, please."

Katrina shook her head. Wasn't the impact of the accident enough? She returned to Marc's room and knocked.

"Come in."

"I can't. I forgot the master key."

A minute later, Marc opened the door. "What happened out there? I heard a crash."

"Tyler hit the floor. Compliments of Ingrid the black belt in judo."

Marc laughed as he tenderly moved back onto the bed. "And I thought it was a party."

"It's heading that way." Maybe she shouldn't have brought him here. "Do you want me to take you back?"

"No, not at all." He stretched his arms over the pillows, taking ownership of the bed and the room and all but inviting Katrina to join him.

Pretending she was unaffected, Katrina sat on the bed, put some rubbing alcohol on a cotton pad, and dabbed at the cut over his forehead. "You're going to have some bruising around the eye."

"Won't be the first time either."

"Seems to be the story of your life."

"The story of any professional athlete's life."

Once his gash stopped bleeding, she put a big bandage over it. "There you go." She put the bandages and the rubbing alcohol back in the first aid kit.

"Is it me, or is it a little chilly in here?"

Oh-oh. "Unfortunately, the weather is playing havoc with the furnace. It's not working at full capacity. Once you're settled, I'll check it. It's not as old as the turnkey but it's also not as new as the TV. It just needs to be reset." She hoped.

He picked up the brass candlestick phone. "Does this work?"

"It did but not right now. We didn't get around to getting phone lines up and running in the bedrooms." It was an outright lie. But she couldn't tell him they cut service to the phones in the guest bedrooms to avoid unnecessary costs. Most guests used their cells, anyway. "I can see about getting it going." Another lie. How could she?

"No need. Can I ask you to get my cell from my coat pocket? It's in the lobby. Here." He took out the swipe key from his pocket and gave it to her. "So you don't have to knock, and I don't have to get up."

Katrina took it and strode back to the lobby with the first aid kit. It was cold in the lobby, too, even though the furnace was at capacity. But there was a big fireplace smack in the center that would warm the room up nicely—if any of her sisters thought about starting it. "Rebeka, can you get a fire going in here?"

Rebeka looked aghast. "You want me to get a fire going? With real wood? You know wood gives me hives."

"Wear gloves."

"I'll still break out."

"I'll do it," Eric said. "I used to start many fires in wood stoves at my grandparents' cabin in Mont Tremblant. Most never burned down things."

How reassuring. "Thank you, Eric." Katrina went into the kitchen. Her sanctuary. No one other than servers and on-call sous chefs bothered her here.

She put the first aid kit back in its spot, took another deep breath to steady herself, and went back into the lobby. Grabbing Marc's coat, she strode to his room, knocked, and let herself in. She hung it in the armoire and gave him his iPhone.

The ice. She forgot the ice. "Back in a minute." She returned to the lobby. Eric and Rebeka stood by the fireplace while the others huddled around them.

"I think I should have watched my grandparents a little more when they got a fire going in their fireplace," Eric said. "I don't know why it hasn't lit by now."

One look told Katrina they piled far too much wood into it. But she kept quiet. Her sisters had never attempted to build a fire, and she didn't have the time to explain it. She'd end up making it herself as she usually did, and Marc needed to ice his foot.

She returned to the kitchen, put ice in a plastic bag, and went back to Marc's room. He had taken off his jacket and tie, unbuttoned his shirt to his chest and looked like a modern-day Adonis on the four-poster bed, speaking into his cell. Now she knew why he was Mr. January. He was big, solid, and chiseled and his profession screamed snow, ice, and January.

"We're all good. We're going to lie low here until the roads are cleared." He listened to the person on the other end of the line. Katrina put the ice on his foot and returned to the lobby. Rebeka read the instructions on how to start a fire from her phone to an attentive crowd.

"Rebeka, can I see you for a moment?" Katrina asked. Rebeka looked at her as though she were an alien. "Can it wait?"

"No, it can't."

Rebeka gave Eric her phone and followed Katrina into the kitchen. "What is it?" She pulled out the elastic around her ponytail and tied it again. "I'm helping Eric start a fire."

"He's a guest before he's Eric. See if he and the other guests want something to eat or drink."

Her eyes widened in horror and she put her hands on her waist, pushing out her ample boobs. "You want me to make something if they do?"

"Offer them something you can make." Which was pretty much nothing edible.

"I'd rather wait until you're ready to prepare something. They're hockey players with deep pockets and fine taste. Did you see their clothes? They didn't buy them at any discount department store. I'm not about to offer them milk and cookies from a package when we could offer them beef bourguignon and some vintage wines."

"I have to start the furnace and make sure Marc isn't hurting more than he's admitting. I don't have time to make them a gourmet meal." She didn't have many ingredients to make a gourmet meal, either.

"They're not going anywhere tonight, Katrina. And I'm sure none of us are shuffling off to bed at 8:00. We have all the time in the world. We'll wait until you have time. I'll offer them a glass of wine in the meantime."

"Fine."

"Any recommendations?"

Of course. She even had to decide on the wine they would enjoy and not her or Marc. "Try one of the Portuguese ports. It's more of a dessert wine but it'll be just the right thing after their near accident. We should have a bottle of a vintage port at the bar."

"What if they want wine? Which one?"

Katrina rolled her eyes. Rebeka was a voracious reader but had no interest in learning about the different kinds of wines or ports. "There's a Zinfandel at the bar, too. It'll be good, but the port might interest them more."

She turned her back on Rebeka before she could ask more questions or make more demands. Times like these, Katrina wished she wasn't the oldest and a chef. Her sisters were inept when it came to the inn. They were more than inept. They just didn't care.

Why couldn't she be like them?

The furnace now. She'd much prefer cooking up a four-course meal from whatever ingredients she had in the kitchen for the hockey guests than going to the sub-basement and tackling the archaic furnace.

She opened the door, flicked on all the lights, and moved down the stairs. They kept supplies in the lower floors, including what was once a vast collection of wines and liqueurs. Many times a day she went up and down the stairs but never to the furnace room.

In the basement, she stared at the old metal door, leading down to the octopus-looking furnace.

Taking a deep breath, she pried it opened, flicked on the light, and moved down the creaking steps. She gulped as she came face to face with the monstrous contraption and its outstretched arms, extending the entire room. "I'm not afraid of you. I'm *not* afraid of you." She moved to the operating panel and flicked several switches as her father did.

But nothing happened.

She tried the switches again.

Still nothing. She banged the furnace.

Nothing.

Shit! Why was this oversized mechanical monstrosity so formidable? She didn't know what else to do short of calling the repairperson and who the heck would come out on a night like tonight?

Defeated, she went back upstairs and to a surprise. Her sisters and the hockey players had a fire going and toasted each other. The opened bottle of the vintage port sat on the coffee table, practically emptied.

"This is delicious," Jakob said.

"It's older than me," Annelise said. "Katrina says the older the wine the better."

"Are you old enough to drink?" he asked.

She pushed up her eyeglasses. With or without them her fair blue eyes lit up her face. "Are you?"

"I'm nineteen."

"So am I."

Thank goodness, Katrina thought. This was a licensed inn and they couldn't serve alcohol to anyone under legal age.

Katrina moved to the big fireplace, took a basket, put some wood in it, and brought it to Marc's room. She was about to knock when she heard Marc.

"I'm not going through any concussion protocol." His voice was taut. "I'm ready to start playing next week as planned. Doctor Harrison all but cleared me yesterday."

She knocked on the door and swiped herself in. Marc's face was red. He resettled himself among the pillows as though he didn't want her to see his agitation. "I'll call first thing in the morning with an update." He abruptly closed his cell. "You're going to build me a fire?" He smiled but the phone call upset him. It was tight.

"The storm is taking its toll. The furnace isn't working, and I don't think I'll be able to convince any repairperson to come out tonight and check it."

The lights blinked on and off several times.

"That may not be the only thing not working soon," Marc said.

"Then I better get this fire going and quickly." She moved the screen aside and piled wood in the fireplace. She lit a twig with a match and placed it under the wood. It took a few moments, but the logs caught on fire. Before long the room lit up in soft patches of heat and warmth.

"I'll bring you some candles in case the electricity goes out." But she hoped it didn't. She'd have to tend the fireplaces in all their rooms during the night and there was no way she could sneak in to keep them going.

"You okay?" Marc asked. "You look far away and lost."

She wiped thoughts of helplessness away. "I caused your accident. You swerved to avoid me. I'm sorry."

"No need to be sorry. You're all right and we're all right. My body has experienced far worse cuts and bruises and thanks to your sisters, the guys shook off any aches or pains. Probably even welcomed them."

"Your car is totaled."

"My insurance will cover the expenses to the car and your wall."

She laughed but without mirth. "I don't think the wall got more than a few nicks. It was built like the fortress walls around a castle by my ancestors. That's why your car suffered more."

Wind rattled the window.

"It wasn't a night to travel," he said.

"You were."

"Yes. But it wasn't supposed to be a blizzard when we left Montreal."

"The weather did take an unusual turn for the worse." She thought about her mother. "Did you see anyone on the road?"

"Nobody since we got onto the road leading to the inn."

If he didn't see any other cars, then her mother was safe somewhere and not driving. Either still at the hospital with her father or at her Aunt Lana's house.

Or maybe she drove and now lay in a ditch confused, cold, and hurt.

"You sure you're all right?"

She nodded but without conviction.

"Do you think you can get one of the guys to get my briefcase from my car? I left my medication in there. I think I'm going to need some painkillers tonight."

Shit. He was more hurt than he let on. "You're really dead, aren't you?"

His smile was sweet. "I'm very much alive. It's just preventative medicine to assure any aches and pains don't turn into lingering problems."

Without saying a word, she went back to the lobby, but her sisters and the hockey guests were gone. Her sisters were probably showing them their rooms.

She grabbed the phone at the front desk and dialed her mother's cell. But there was no answer. She tried the hospital and asked for her father's room. No answer there, either.

A worse thought than her mother driving on the road took hold of her. What if her father had suffered another heart attack? What if he really was on his last breath?

No, she couldn't think of worse-case scenarios. Phone lines or cell towers were down. That was all. Otherwise, her mother would call.

No news was good news. She had to keep it in mind.

Marc needed his medication. She didn't want to go back out in the blizzard, but she had no choice.

She put on her parka, hat, boots, and gloves. Ice was building around the roof, veranda, and trees. The snow was higher, too. Fighting wind and snow and sleet, she made it to the car. All the doors stood open.

She grabbed the briefcase from the floor in the back, closed undamaged or unfrozen doors, and went back inside. She locked the inn's door and removed the winter wear. Her face was cold. She touched her cheeks. They felt frozen.

She was about to head to Marc's room when she saw a bottle of their finest cognac. Maybe he'd prefer a shot or two of the cognac to painkillers. She grabbed the bottle and a snifter and, with the briefcase, returned to Marc's room.

Marc flinched at the sight of her face. "Did you go outside to get it?"

"The others were in their rooms."

"You look frostbitten. I would have done without the painkillers."

"I'm fine. I thought a little cognac might make the pain go away a lot better than your painkillers." She held up the briefcase and the cognac.

Marc went white. She was now more than afraid. She started to panic. "You are dead, I knew it." How the hell would she get him to a hospital?

"You might wish me dead, very soon, Katrina." He raised himself against the pillows. "You've been very good to me. Too good as a matter of fact."

"It's my job."

"No, you've gone beyond the call of duty. You are an angel and I owe my angel the truth." He swallowed, which made Katrina nervous again. "We were headed here tonight."

"Unfortunately, the restaurant is closed."

"That's okay. You wouldn't have served me."

Katrina scowled. "I don't understand."

"Do you have any knives on you?"

She was now really confused.

"I'm the CEO of King Court Development."

Katrina felt the blood drain from her face. "You mean the company that wants to buy my inn and restaurant and tear them down?"

He nodded. "My medication is in the briefcase. But I also brought the papers I need you to sign in case you wanted to sell to me tonight. They're in there, too."

Katrina couldn't breathe. She couldn't even move. Then she let the briefcase fall right on Marc's swollen foot.

Chapter Five

Marc squirmed, winced, and kicked the briefcase off his foot. "Now it may be broken. Excuse me. Ow! That hurt."

Anger raged inside her like the blizzard outside. She couldn't find the words to express herself. "I brought you the papers you wanted me to sign," she pointed to the briefcase, "in that—thing?"

He put the ice back on his ankle. "If you remember, I did ask you to get one of the guys to get it. And you have the papers. They're the same I emailed your lawyer earlier this week."

She slammed the bottle of cognac on the night table along with the snifter. "So, all that—discomfort after I told you who I was and all the business about not throwing knives and wanting one of the guys to help you. It was simply a cover-up to not tell me who you really were and why you were here?"

Marc considered it. "Well, yes."

Katrina's anger broke through. "And to think I drooled all over you."

"You did?" He flashed a boyish smile. "I'm flattered."

"You mean no other woman has drooled over you?"

"It's always been anything but a drool."

"You're so full of yourself. The drooling is

47

finished." She barged out of the room and slammed the door shut.

"But I wasn't expecting you to sign them today. I was only being proactive." Katrina heard him say. "I came to speak face to face. As you requested. But brought the papers just in case you were ready to sign." He shouted his last words, but she heard them all. Loud and clear.

Katrina strode into the kitchen and to the pantry. She pulled out the flour and sugar and threw them on the marble counter. From the fridge she took the eggs, milk, yeast, and butter. She washed her hands, threw on her apron, and in a bowl put in the dry ingredients, mixing them with a whisk She added four eggs, one by one, the milk and when it clumped together, she used her hands to crumble in the butter. Once it was a mishmash, she scattered flour on the countertop, plopped the dough onto it, and kneaded.

He was the CEO of King Court Development. He was the one who wanted to buy her family's inn, her restaurant, and the entire property. He was the one who wanted to tear everything down—over one hundred and fifty years of love and labor—since Canada became a country—and build townhouses, stretching all the way from the road to the far corners of the property. *He* was the one who refused to do what she wanted.

She punched the dough on the counter.

He was the one who wanted to do away with history and reinvent the property.

She kneaded and slapped the dough.

He was the one who would prove to the world how terrible her plan to modernize the inn and restaurant were. She was so inept.

She kneaded until it was soft and smooth.

He was the one who wanted to kick her and her parents out.

She tucked the dough together to form a ball.

He was the bad guy dressed, oh so impeccably, as the good guy.

She threw the dough into a bowl, covered it with plastic, and set it on the stove.

He was the one who was so damn gorgeous. He made her pant like a foolish thirteen-year-old girl.

From the fridge, she took out the leftover pork shoulder from the curling championship luncheon. She heated the drippings and shredded the meat. She grabbed the last four baguettes she baked that morning from the pantry. She cut three of the baguettes in sections and added a mound of the pulled pork, along with the warm drippings. She took the coleslaw from the fridge and topped the sandwiches.

She couldn't believe she brought him the documents that needed her signature to sell him her entire life and history and to kick her out on the street.

She topped each sandwich with another slice of baguette and arranged the sandwiches on a platter along with the summer's preserved pickles and dried olives. On a tray, she put the remainder of the coleslaw, the plates, some napkins, and the cutlery.

He couldn't walk to the lobby without her assistance to eat. His poor ankle was bruised. She'd have to bring him his food.

She'd make him starve.

That's right. She'd play bad and not offer him food. She'd show him she was no angel. Her own sisters wouldn't recognize her or match her. No more nice and dutiful and polite Katrina Sherrer. No more honey or angel, either. She was going to the dark side and staying there.

She grabbed another plate. For Marc. Dammit! She was an angel. Why couldn't she be a fallen angel and let him crawl to the lobby and the food?

She took the last baguette, sliced it into thin pieces, and put them on another tray with a plate, napkin, fork, and knife. From the fridge, she removed pâté and brie. She was about to add one of the pulled pork sandwiches on the tray but decided against it. She could be a fallen angel in training and give him a taste of food. If he was hungry, he'd have to get off the bed, hobble to the lobby, and get himself a sandwich.

There. Not a bad start to being bad.

She brought the platter of sandwiches to the lobby and set it on the coffee table in front of the fireplace, followed by the tray with the coleslaw and plates.

Her sisters and the hockey players laughed from somewhere near their rooms. Laughing could only lead to one thing. Carnal pleasures as her grandmother used to say after watching one of her steamy soap operas. Carnal pleasures was the short-lived joy but ultimate ruin of all her favorite characters.

From the front desk, Katrina grabbed a handful of condoms. Guests often asked for them. She slapped them next to the tray of sandwiches. She had done her duty to her father. She had told her sisters no sex under his roof. The rest was in her sisters' hands.

She stared at the condoms. All those condoms made it seem she approved of a whole lot of sex. She didn't care, but why give her sisters all the enjoyment? She wasn't partaking in any of the fun.

She grabbed a few condoms and stuck them in her jacket pocket. She covered the ones on the tray with the napkins and returned to the kitchen. She took the other tray to Marc's room and banged on the door with her foot. She had the swipe card but refused to use it. Let the bad guy hobble in pain to the door. There was some shuffling and the door opened.

"Katrina—"

She brushed past him. She could serve him, but she didn't have to either look or talk to him. He was the enemy and admitted it. She was about to place the tray on the coffee table in front of the fireplace, but the briefcase was there. Inside were those sacrilegious documents. Once signed they would rob her of her life and future. She put the tray on the night table. "There are sandwiches and salad in the lobby. You want some, you'll have to use your feet to get them."

"Katrina—"

"Pâté or brie?"

"Katrina—"

"Pâté or brie?"

"Pâté." He moved onto the bed.

She took a couple slices of bread, spread pâté on them, put them on a plate, and handed it to him. He took the plate and pulled himself higher against the headboard.

Music came from the lobby. "Sounds like they're now really having a party out there."

"Stand up and get yourself there if you want to join them."

"I wasn't insinuating I wanted to go." He took a bite of the pâté. "This is delicious."

"Of course."

"Imported from France?"

Her gaze shot needles into him.

He held up the bread and pâté. "You made these?"

"Everything you're eating." She pulled the top off the cognac. "The pâté, brie, baguette, and the sandwiches and salad in the lobby along with the preserves."

"You're a cook?"

Her mouth dropped open. "I'm a cordon bleu chef, trained in Ottawa, Paris, and New York. I've helped prepare dinners for the prime minister and visiting dignitaries." She didn't play humble when it came to her cooking. She was one of the best chefs. She was offered jobs around the world but chose to create her own style at the Acadia Restaurant. She wished now she had chosen one of those jobs. She wouldn't face the loss of the only thing she wanted.

"My apologies." He positioned the pillows more comfortably. "Then I suppose you are the chef of the restaurant here."

She poured him some cognac. "It certainly isn't any of my three wayward sisters." She wanted to use the past tense but didn't.

"It must receive many good reviews."

She handed him the snifter. "Exceptional reviews." *A top-caliber, fine nouveau French restaurant with a twist of rustic First Nations cuisine, set in a historical country-side inn* was the review from one of the top gastronomical magazines. *Nothing like this kind of cuisine anywhere in Canada. One of a kind. Simple but sublime.* "Until everything went to pot, and I resorted to what most customers who came this way wanted. Hamburgers, ribs, and fries."

Marc put the plate on the bed and took the snifter. "I'm sure they were the best hamburgers, ribs, and fries any of your customers ate."

Katrina scowled. "Stop the flattery. It didn't work before, and it isn't working now, either."

"They weren't the best hamburgers, ribs, and fries?"

Katrina wasn't in the mood to spar. "They were the damn best." Until customers stopped coming. Why would customers trek all the way from Ottawa or the surrounding area when they could get adequate fast and fatty food close to home? She strode to the window to hide her shame and drew a curtain aside. The snow covered most of the flower pots she forgot to bring to the barns and more came down. She remembered her parents and her sadness and anger evaporated. She hoped her mother wasn't on the road and her father was all right. She would call again if she didn't hear from them soon.

"This is a magnificent cognac. It's the best I've ever had. You didn't make this, did you?"

She yanked the curtains closed. "I could, but I don't have a license. The one you're drinking is over thirty years old."

"It must cost a fortune."

"It's going on your tab." She moved to the side of his bed. "Would you like anything else, Mr. CEO?"

"It's Marc." He patted the side of the bed. "Sit down, Katrina. Let's talk."

She grabbed a slice of bread and spread brie on it. "There's nothing to talk about."

"Then why did you request a face to face meeting?"

"False hope and stupidity."

"I don't think so. I came as you requested, so let's talk."

"You should have called before you came. My lawyer would be here with me, and I wouldn't be stuck alone with you, trying to play nice when I want to throw the pillows in your face."

Marc smirked. "Would the pillows hurt me?"

"Would you prefer the knives?"

Marc squirmed. "I did call. But no one answered. There wasn't even voice mail."

Katrina pulled out her cell. Shit. It wasn't on. She opened it, but the battery was dead. The corners of his lips turned up. He was amused but she wasn't. "You should have sent a pigeon."

"They all went south."

He kept his gaze on her, waiting for her to say something, but she only spewed anger.

"I did what you wanted me to do, Katrina. Now talk to me. What did you want to say that couldn't be said over the phone or in an email?"

Katrina handed him the bread with the brie. Should she, or shouldn't she? Emotions clogged her throat like sour bile. She didn't know whether the words would come out coherently. But he came. He did as she asked. She didn't have anything to lose. "I wanted to show you what you wanted to destroy. A hundred and fifty years of history." *A hundred and fifty years of her family's history* she wanted to add but remained silent.

Marc took the bread with brie and put it on his plate. "I'm buying the inn and property to make money. The inn won't make me any money even with the additions you suggested." He sighed. "Unfortunately, its history is at its end."

Katrina was told the same more often than she wanted to hear and remained silent. It was easy for him to say it. It was always easier to speak of a loss when it wasn't one's own.

"You're close to bankruptcy, creditors are banging on your door, and the banks aren't giving out any more loans."

She moved toward the fireplace, not wanting to show him the humiliation and pain on her face. "You've got a good team of lawyers and investigators."

"It became public knowledge when you listed the inn and property. You can recover some of your losses by selling to me. What I'm offering you will provide very well for you and your sisters and your parents. I believe your father has two brothers who'll also get a good share. Everything you have in the inn will bring in quite a lot. If you go into bankruptcy, you'll lose everything."

"I'm well aware." Her voice was a murmur. How could a once viable and prosperous inn become so desolate? It was incomprehensible.

She added a log to the fireplace and watched as licks of fire engulfed it.

"So, what happened, Katrina? The inn did very well to survive one hundred and fifty years."

"For a hundred and forty-five years." She stopped. She didn't want to tell him more.

"Then?" His tone was encouraging and not at all insulting.

She took a deep breath. "Then two other resorts opened in the area. Both offered skiing, snowboarding, swimming slides, golf, and family entertainment to name only a few things. Families with kids don't want to spend a romantic evening in a historic five-star inn, eating a gourmet meal, and drinking fine cognac in front of a fireplace. Chicken fingers and coke in your every day lodge with indoor swimming slides and outdoor snow-tubing is more enticing and cost efficient."

He indicated the room. "But everything looks new or well-kept anyway."

"My father refurbished the furniture, renovated the guest rooms, and made the lobby larger. He spent money in the wrong places. He should have put in ski lifts and a golf course or a water park and a family-friendly entertainment center. He should have set us up to compete with the two other lodges."

"Why didn't he?"

She moved the logs with the poker. "He wanted to stay true to the original concept of the inn. I bought into it. I thought it had a chance of working."

She put the poker back on the stand, moved the screen over the fireplace, and dusted off some debris from her hands. She should have dissuaded her father and convinced him of the necessity of modernizing the inn and making it attractive to families with children and not renovating and making it true to its history. She should have fought him until he understood it was wrong, but she was selfish and her attempts half-hearted. The modernizations would make them competitive, but they would also entail every day, diner-style food. The renovations he made, however, were in line with the set-up of her restaurant and its nouveau cuisine. She could picture the reviews. A five-star inn housing a future three-star restaurant. A quaint inn coupled with a romantic restaurant and cuisine. It was perfect. It was everything she dreamed of and wanted.

Then the dream caved in around them. No one came. No guests. No customers. No one wanted romance. They wanted entertainment. No one wanted exceptional cuisine. They wanted burgers. They lost money and more money until there were only worries, fears, and finally grief.

She couldn't believe how naïve, self-centered, and dreamy-eyed she was. The decision took a toll on her father's health, the family's well-being, and their livelihood. It resulted in their present state of near bankruptcy—of destitute if they didn't sell, and in his ill-health. Her dream of a five-star inn housing a future three-star restaurant blew up in her face. She was as much at fault for the demise of the inn and restaurant as her parents. It was something she still couldn't believe.

"I'm sorry, Katrina." Marc's voice was barely a whisper, but it shook her with its warmth.

She didn't want his understanding but appreciated it. "So am I." She took another deep breath. "If you came here, I hoped I could show you the inn and property." She waited and was thankful. There was no ridicule in his eyes but compassion. "I hoped to show you the land, present you with my proposal of what could make it viable and competitive again, and then you could make your decision. The Acadia Inn really is one of a kind in Ontario and in Canada."

Marc took a sip of the cognac. "As my lawyer informed yours, your proposal has merit and could in the long run make the inn thrive again, but it's not cost-efficient or profitable for me in the short run. It's far more lucrative to build townhouses and starter homes."

She strode to the bed. "So, go find another piece of property and let me find someone who will fall in love with my proposal and bow eternally to me for making it."

Marc laughed. "In other words, you want me to do your bidding."

"Yes."

He shook his head. "I'd do any other bidding for you except this. This is the best site, Katrina. It's only a half hour to an hour away from Ottawa. Families could easily commute from the city to their homes. There'd be townhouses, so they'd be affordable to first time home owners and single-family homes for those who are established. I build here, and I'm set for life and so will the people investing with me. It's not just me who gains from the investment."

"How did you even come across this area?"

His eyebrows shot up. "I'm Mr. January Hockey Player, remember? I was born and raised here in King Court, just like you were."

"Don't you make enough money playing hockey? You professional athletes make millions in one season and even more millions with sponsorships. I've seen you in those sportswear commercials—in your tight tops and shorts and in some beer commercials and even in the ads for some new sports store."

He picked up the slice of bread with brie. "I'm closing in on retirement."

"Really? At the ripe old age of what—thirtyish?"

"I'm thirty-one. A hockey player might make it to thirty-eight if he's good, but most retire by thirty-six."

"So you still have a few more years before you

have to retire. Find some other prime property that will bring in your ultra-millions and let the god of country-side inns bring me another multi-millionaire who will praise my proposal and meekly bend to my will. What the heck are you going to do with all those multi-millions, anyway? Buy your own hockey team?"

"Maybe," he said with a slight smile.

The lights flicked off and on.

She waited to see if they would go on and off again. Nothing. "You can't buy one now?"

He seemed reticent to answer.

"There you go. You don't need to build houses on my property to become a multi-millionaire and get yourself a team. You can afford it already. You could even do my bidding and remain a multi-millionaire."

Marc laughed as the lights flickered again. "Looks like we might be continuing this discussion in the dark, Katrina."

The lights went out, leaving them in darkness.

"Correction. Looks like we *are* continuing this discussion in the dark."

Chapter Six

The door! Katrina raced to it and turned the knob. Nothing. "No!" She couldn't get stuck in this bedroom with Mr. CEO King Court Development aka Mr. January Hockey Player. He wasn't compliant. He was her arch enemy, and she didn't want him to be anything else.

He was also damn gorgeous and alluring, and she didn't trust herself from falling all over him. And more!

"The doors work on electricity?"

"We had to ensure guests would be safe inside their rooms if there was a power outage." She pulled at it, tugged it, banged on it, and kicked it. This could not be happening.

"Would it really be so bad being stuck with me in this bedroom?"

The lights came back on, saving her the trouble of answering a question she had no proper answer for. "Don't move."

"Wouldn't think of it," he replied with a sly smile. "But you didn't answer my question."

Katrina pulled a "I-am-not-about-to-answer-that" grin and strode out and to the lobby where the fireplace roared. The lights sputtered again. She had to find some flashlights and candles and put them in the hockey players' rooms. She also needed a good flashlight for herself.

Her sisters and the hockey players raced from the opposite side of the inn.

"We need candles, Katrina," Ingrid said, moving past her. "Hey. Sandwiches. Any one hungry?"

"Always," Eric replied. They gathered around the coffee table in front of the fireplace, helped themselves to the sandwiches and coleslaw, and forgot about the candles.

"This looks good," Tyler said, grabbing a sandwich.

"Katrina is a chef," Rebeka replied.

"Mm, this tastes good." Tyler gave Katrina a thumbs-up.

Katrina went to the kitchen, threw flashlights and candles in a bag, and brought them to her sisters.

"This is the best pulled pork sandwich I've ever had, Katrina," Jakob said. "Tastes like it was slowly barbequed for hours."

"It was," Katrina replied.

"I'm not a fan of cabbage but I could eat this coleslaw all by myself," Tyler said.

Eric pulled the coleslaw closer. "You're not."

"Katrina can make more if we run out," Rebeka said.

Of course, Katrina could, she thought. Their wish was her command—but not her sisters' command. She put a flashlight in front of each of her sisters along with candles and matches. "In case the lights go out, you'll need these to bring our guests to their rooms."

"Won't the backup generator kick in?" Annelise asked, taking some olives.

Katrina glared her sister down until she understood what she meant.

"If the lights go out, we'll just stay down here around this fire and have a party," Jakob said.

"Do we have any dessert?" Tyler asked, eating away at his sandwich.

"What would you like?" Annelise asked. "Katrina can make anything but her bittersweet chocolate soufflé with espresso sauce is sinful."

"I'm a sinning kind of guy," Tyler said. "Bring it on, Katrina."

Katrina was on her way to Marc's room and stopped. "I'm afraid there isn't any kind of soufflé on the menu today. We have ice cream if you're interested."

"Ice cream in the middle of winter?" Ingrid said.

Katrina leveled a frosty glare colder than any ice cream.

"Ice cream is good," Ingrid said with a small smile.

"What flavors do you have?" Eric asked.

"I made tiramisu and white brownie chocolate."

"Both," everyone replied at once.

"Can I have mine in a waffle cone?" Ingrid asked.

"I don't have time to make waffle cones," Katrina replied, doing her best to sweeten her voice.

"Can you at least fix them for us? You always add something and make it even yummier."

Yes, she was the yummy chef. Bless her culinary certificates. Right now, however, she wished she could just scoop the ice cream from a pre-packaged container and stick a no-name chocolate chip cookie in it.

Stifling her irritation, she went back to the kitchen, took out six champagne glasses, added a scoop of both ice cream flavors and topped them with a coffee liqueur sauce and a chocolate *tuile*. She brought them out on a tray and set it on the coffee table.

"I usually just eat ice cream straight from the container," Jakob said. "This is nice. Thank you."

No one had lifted the napkins hiding the condoms. Good. Served them right fueling the culinary pleasures of the stomach and forgetting about the carnal pleasures of the flesh.

For now. The night—or rather the party—was just starting.

The lights blinked off and on several times.

"I have to bring this flashlight and some candles to Marc's room." She looked at each of her sisters. "Please take the plates back to the kitchen and put them in the dishwasher when you're finished."

"For sure. All right. Not a problem," were the various replies. But Katrina knew she'd find them on the coffee table in the morning.

At Marc's door, she knocked. When she heard him say to come in, she swiped the card and entered. She placed a flashlight on the night table for easy access and put candles around the room.

"Can we continue talking now?" Marc asked.

"I've said everything I have to say. You know why I wanted you to come but you're not interested. There's no use in arguing my point."

The lights flickered and went out. Katrina held her breath. Were they going to come back on? *Please, come back on,* she prayed. *Please.*

Nothing.

Katrina waited. Her gaze fell on the door and so did Marc's. His smile turned wicked. Hers turned desperate.

"No." Her voice was a squeak. "This can't be."

Marc flicked the flashlight on her and held up the bottle. "Cognac?"

Chapter Seven

Marc couldn't pull his gaze from Katrina. Since she all but dragged him from the car, he tried to put her together but without success. Probably because her hard-as-nails, take-charge exterior, and the I-don't-have-time and don't-give-me-shit attitude made him sit up and listen. Tall and willowy with errant blonde hair, which even pulled back in a tight ponytail curled at leisure around her face, Katrina was a puzzle to piece together. But every time he found one piece that looked like it would fit into another and give him insight into her, he was wrong.

He needed to figure her out. How could a woman who kept telling him, in her own words, she didn't like him and his ego, cause such excitement in him? It didn't make sense. *She* didn't make sense and he needed her to make sense. What was it about her that riled his curiosity and made him wonder what she would look like without her dark workout gear on, her ponytail untied, and nice words sprouting out of her lovely lips? He wouldn't even mind hearing some choice dirty words coming out of her lips as long as it came with foreplay.

But right now, for such an ethereal-looking woman, she had a set of lungs, which would work magic rounding-up sheep in the mountains. She banged at the door, calling each of her sisters, demanding they acknowledge her. But music blared from the lobby. No one would hear her except some stranded sheep caught up in the blizzard.

"You can scream all you want but they can't hear you." He wanted to say they probably didn't want to hear her, but the fear of a tirade made him keep his thoughts to himself. Not that he was afraid of a tirade from her. He looked forward to it, even wanted it. No woman's tirade would arouse him more than Katrina's. Everything about her aroused his interest—and so much more.

But he'd keep the thought also to himself. She wasn't in the mood to spar with him. "The cognac is—" He wanted to say the cognac would calm her down but decided against it. "The cognac is smooth and silky. Come and have some."

She pulled out her cell but threw it on the floor. In a huff she stuffed it back in her pocket. "Can I borrow your cell?"

He held it out to her. She punched in some numbers, frowned, punched in more numbers, and screamed in frustration. "I can't remember any of my sisters' numbers."

Maybe if she calmed down, she would. Yet another thought he wasn't about to say out loud. She was one interesting woman. That thought, too, he'd keep to himself.

He took the phone and called Eric who picked up after several rings. "Katrina would like to speak to one of her sisters, please." Marc put the phone on speaker.

"Hello?"

"Ingrid, it's me," Katrina said. "I'm stuck in Marc's room. Can you come and try opening the door from the outside?"

Ingrid laughed. "Katrina's stuck in Marc's room."

Everyone laughed. A lot. Marc tried not to join in and stifled a grin.

"Lucky guy," Tyler shouted.

"Get me out of here," Katrina yelled.

"Hold on," Ingrid said.

They waited until they heard footsteps and voices at the door. Someone jostled the doorknob. "You're right. It's stuck," Eric said.

Katrina fisted her hands.

"Keep trying," Marc said. He had to support the cause—for Katrina's sake and took a sip of cognac.

They all banged, hit, kicked, and swore at the door, rattling only the washstand and making Katrina pace back and forth.

"If all three of us run into the door with our shoulders," Marc heard Jakob say, "then maybe it will cave in."

"You mean like the police detectives do on TV?" one of Katrina's sisters said.

"Exactly."

"Go for it."

"Stand back, Katrina," Jakob said. "Big men at work."

Katrina moved away as Marc shook his head. The door was made of real wood, not particle board. They would dislocate their shoulders.

He crossed his legs and took another sip of cognac. There was a big bang at the door. It shook the TV on the wall. Three men cried out in pain. Marc settled himself better on the bed to keep himself from laughing.

"The door is a fortress," Eric said.

"Sorry," Tyler said. "Looks like you're having your own private party in there until the power comes back on."

"No, don't go." Katrina banged on the door. "Find a screwdriver and take the door down."

"Where's the screwdriver?" one of her sisters asked. He was sure it was Annelise.

"In the basement."

Silence.

"It's dark," Annelise said. "You know I don't go to the basement after dark."

Marc's eyebrows rose in disbelief.

"Please, Annelise," Katrina said. "Take the guys and go down there."

"Not me. Even with bodyguards."

"Ingrid? Rebeka?" Katrina said.

"Sorry," both replied.

"It's spooky down there especially when there aren't any lights," Rebeka said.

"It's spooky down there even with lights," Ingrid added.

"You have company," Katrina said. "I'm sure the guys could swat a spider if one came your way."

"Those guys wouldn't know a screwdriver from a wooden spoon," Marc said.

Even with just the flashlight on, Marc saw Katrina's face turning red with frustration. What a turn on. He wanted to strip her clothes off now. An angel with the passion of a devil.

Too bad she wasn't interested. She said she didn't like him. Marc didn't care what other women thought about him, even if they were spending the night together. But with Katrina, what she thought of him mattered. It baffled him.

"Have a good evening," Tyler said. "Be good, Marc."

"Be nice, Katrina," Rebeka said.

Footsteps moved away. Katrina banged at the door again. "Come back. Who's going to feed you?" It didn't seem she was ready to admit defeat. Music came from the lobby again, sealing her defeat. She turned to face him. Marc did the only thing he could do. He patted the bed and held up the bottle of cognac. "I saw a glass in the bathroom."

Katrina grabbed it and came forward as though she were in a death march. She slapped it on the night table and fumed. Marc poured her a glass of cognac, but she wouldn't take it. "Time to enjoy a night cap and let it take all your stress away. Or is that what you're afraid of?"

She pulled herself to her full height. "I'm not afraid to relax."

"Good. Then take it and be nice to me."

"Professionally nice?"

"It's a start."

She grabbed the glass, fell into the chair, drank it in one shot and held it out for him to refill. Marc dutifully obeyed.

"You're not going to have any more?" she asked.

"I'd love to, but I think I need my meds, now. Could you get them for me, please? They're in my briefcase. My head is swimming."

She put the glass down and went to his briefcase. She gasped. "You take all of these? There must be eight different containers."

"No, some are Tyler's, and some are Eric's. Most are vitamins or minerals and believe it or not, Jakob's sinus medication. The one with the orange top is mine. Two please."

She took two out and used his snifter to get water from the bathroom. He popped both pills into his mouth and swallowed them with a good gulp of water. He lay back against the pillow and watched as she lit some candles. Holding the flashlight, she moved to the window and drew the curtains aside. Ice glistened in the dark, but trees swayed, and snow fell and whirled around. The window shook with the wind.

Marc thought the window would shatter, but Katrina seemed oblivious. Her thoughts were elsewhere. "Are you expecting guests tonight?"

"We aren't expecting guests until April."

"Then what are you looking for?"

"My mother might be out there." She was about to take out her cell when she remembered it wasn't working.

"Use mine."

"It's not necessary. I'm sure she's waiting out the storm somewhere safe."

"What's her number?"

"Really—"

She was so obstinate. "What's her number?"

With a sigh of resignation, she took the phone and punched in the number but there was no answer. She handed it back to him. "I'll try again later."

"Does your father have a cell?"

"He does but he's not using it right now."

"Not using it right now?" Marc waited for more information.

"My mother took him to the hospital earlier today. My father had a heart attack six months ago. He's had complications ever since especially with water in his lungs. He can't answer if he's going through thoracentesis, the procedure to remove it."

He held the phone out for her again. "Try the hospital."

Katrina didn't move from the window. "It's not necessary."

What a stubborn woman. "What hospital is he at?"

She grimaced. "Ottawa Civic. Wilhelm Sherrer."

Marc found the number and put the phone on speaker. The receptionist gave him her father's room and a woman answered.

Katrina bolted to the bed. "Mom, are you okay?"

"Yes, I am, Katrina." She sounded exhausted.

"You need to stay put. It's really bad out there."

"I've been told. You're okay?"

"We're fine. We got some unexpected guests. We're taking care of them. But we lost power about half an hour ago."

"Oh dear. And the generator won't kick in. It hasn't been serviced."

"I know." She glanced at Marc, but he had guessed and shrugged it off.

"I've got the guests in the rooms with the fireplaces."

"That's a lot of work to keep them going. You can't tend to them during the night while they're sleeping."

"I know but it's the only option for now. How's Dad?"

Her mom remained silent. Katrina's face went pale,

making Marc sit up.

"Mom?"

"The doctors are removing water from his lungs as we speak."

"But he'll be okay?"

"He should be but they're taking a long time. It was faster the first time."

"He's weaker now. I'm sure they have to be more careful."

"Maybe." But she didn't sound convinced.

"Call me when he comes back to his room. My cell isn't working. Call anyone else."

"I will. Your sisters are okay, then?"

"Yes. The guests are hockey players from Dad's favorite team, Montreal. Ingrid, Rebeka and Annelise are excited, to say the least."

Her mother laughed but without spirit. "I'll make sure and tell your father. It'll incite him to get better. Take some photos and get them to sign his hockey stick. I think it's in the basement."

"I will. Be careful, Mom, and tell Dad," she glanced at Marc, "tell him we're thinking about him." Marc closed his phone. "Thank you."

Throughout the conversation with her mother, it became clear to Marc why Katrina was protective of the inn. "If you sell the inn and property to me and I tear them down as I intend to, you're afraid your father won't recover."

Katrina picked up the glass and slumped back into the chair. She didn't say anything for a long minute. "Yes."

Marc spread some pâté on a slice of bread and gave it to her.

She was surprised. "I should be serving you."

"I can't serve you? Try it. It's delicious. I can attest to it."

She took it but hesitantly.

He spread more pâté on another slice of bread. "You have legal signing authority. Your parents put the responsibility of selling the inn in your hands." He took a bite. "Why?"

Katrina held the bread in one hand, but it seemed she wasn't aware of it. "When my parents put the inn up for sale, my dad had a heart attack and my mother's blood pressure shot off the scale. We thought she would have a heart attack, too. When my dad recovered, they put the fate of the inn and property in my hands. Neither he nor my mother was capable of making any decisions. Neither was physically healthy nor mentally strong. But it had to be done. It was the least I could do for them."

"And you?"

Katrina's eyebrows lifted as though she was surprised by the question.

"How are you faring with the weight of selling your livelihood and home on your shoulders?"

Katrina almost laughed. "You can't tell?"

Marc made himself more comfortable. "Angry, disillusioned, sad, very sad." He wanted to say he thought she was close to grieving, but it was too emotional. It was her home and her livelihood, too. He appeared heartless to her, but he wasn't. He understood loss.

Katrina twirled the glass, keeping her eyes on the golden liquid.

Marc took a bite of the pâté. Katrina was

uncomfortable—more than uncomfortable. She couldn't respond. It was time to change the subject, especially when he was the one who wanted to take it all away. "I've done a lot of traveling and I've eaten at some of the finest and most expensive restaurants all over the world, but this is the best pâté and bread I've ever had. You're better than good. You're exceptional."

"Like I said. I'm a cordon bleu chef. I learned from the best."

"You could be making a fortune at any three-star restaurant."

"Before the ribs and hot dogs, the Acadia Restaurant was on its way to getting a star rating." She took a sip of the cognac. "My cuisine was referred to as a fusion of modern French, Acadian, and First Nations. We had a cook here once, not even a chef, and she took her inspiration from what she found in the forests, lakes, and hills around here. She belonged to a reserve not too far from the inn. I often went with her while she 'sniffed around' as she would say. I learned a lot from her, including some interesting techniques. She passed away just before I went to culinary school. I think she would have approved of my cuisine." She took a sip of the cognac. "The restaurant was the only thing carrying us."

"Then?"

"Then the other two lodges popped up and we had to cut corners and begin catering to the same customers. Before I knew it, I was juggling gourmet meals with fast food. Then, nobody came for the fine cuisine and we cut that out, too. Needless to say, it cut into me." She took a sip of her cognac. "We used to book weddings, but we didn't this year. We didn't know if we'd still be around. I do the occasional catering now and again but not enough to carry us. You may have figured it out by now, but we've cut other corners—many other corners. We cut the phone lines several months ago and, as you heard, there is no working generator."

He chewed the pâté as he considered her predicament. "I'm sure you've thought about what you'd do if the inn closed down. Any restaurant would scoop you up."

"The last thing I've thought about is what I'm going to do once the inn is sold. It would be hard starting out as a line or sous chef again." She took another sip of the cognac. "I'd probably clash with the head chef. I'd be more qualified—and probably better—than him or her. As you can see, I've got a bit of an ego, too."

"And you shouldn't be ashamed. You could open up another restaurant."

"Once I pay off our creditors, give my uncles their share of the property, which amounts to half of whatever we have left, make sure my parents are settled for retirement, and give my sisters their share, I'm afraid there won't be enough left for me to do anything."

"You need to take your cut."

She pulled her legs up to her chest, looking for the first time both at ease but like a lost little girl. She still hadn't taken a bite of the bread and placed it on the plate. "I want my cut to be used for the debts. And then I want everyone settled. I'm last on the totem pole."

"That's very big sister of you but your sisters are adults. I'm sure they can take care of themselves without big sis looking out for them. From what I can make out, they seem to have already moved on."

Katrina took a while before answering. "Ingrid just started working as a lawyer for a corporate law firm in Toronto. Rebeka is a high school science teacher in Ottawa, and Annelise is studying engineering at the University of Ottawa. They were smart. Smarter than me. They never wanted anything to do with the inn." She took another sip. "It's just me. I can't seem to let go." She took a while before answering. "Everything I wanted was here. Creative license to create my own style of food and the ambiance in a five-star inn. Out there, I would be a nobody. I would have to start at the bottom and prove my abilities, something I'm not looking forward to."

"But you won't be there for long. You'd build yourself up quickly. You're good."

"I probably would, but I can't do that again, Marc, when I've been at the top."

"Do I hear an ego rivaling my own?"

Katrina smirked. "Yes, I had a big one at one time, too. You can't make it to the top of your business without one."

He held up his snifter of water. "Hear, hear. You accuse me of too much pride and self-importance, but you understand me."

Her smile was sly. "I have to keep some secrets to myself."

"Of course." Even though he wanted to hear all of them. "I'm offering you quite a bit. There will be enough for you, too. Especially when you sell everything you have inside the inn."

She bowed her head and for a moment Marc

thought she was crying. He felt lower than a rat. He made her feel terrible.

"You don't know how much we owe." She put her feet down and leaned forward. It was the first time she looked at him honestly, without anger or fear or anxiety. It was as though he could read what she wanted to say without her saying it. His heart pounded. She was lost. Completely and utterly lost.

Just like he would be without hockey in his life. And why he needed to buy the inn and the land around it. He had never been without anything. He had never been a nobody. He needed to show everyone he could survive without hockey. He could still be a force to be reckoned with.

"Why can't you just buy the inn and property and keep it as it is, including the restaurant? Add in the golf course and water parks for kids and add another restaurant to appeal to a kid's palate. It could all work."

"You want to flip burgers for me?"

"I just don't want anything destroyed. Everything is so precious. I could run the gourmet restaurant and flip burgers for you."

"The property screams housing development. It screams money. Those guys out there with your sisters are investing with me along with several others. The profit won't only be mine. Even if I back off, they won't, and another development company will rush in and offer you a lower price. Other development companies came knocking, didn't they?" She didn't acknowledge, which gave him the answer. "They see the viability and lucrativeness of building homes on this property. This is my retirement package. It's theirs, too."

"You're not retiring tomorrow."

Marc shifted. "No, but I want to be prepared. I was off most of the last hockey season with a concussion I couldn't shake. Three weeks ago, I suffered another one. It's not as big as the one last year, but it's made me rethink my life. So, you see, I do understand how it would feel to give up what you love, Katrina. Hockey has been my life since my father gave me a hockey stick just after I learned to walk, added blades to the bottom of my boots, put me on an ice rink, and made me play with him and my older brother. It's in my blood, just like the inn is in yours. But the concussions have forced me to think beyond hockey. Sometimes, we just have to move on whether our egos like it or not. Whether our egos want to or not. Whether our egos are ready or not."

Chapter Eight

Katrina added the last log to the fire. The power was still out but she checked the door anyway. If it didn't come back soon, she wouldn't have any more logs to keep the room warm.

Her sisters and the guys laughed and talked. Their voices carried all the way from the lobby and over the salsa music they played.

"They're having a good time," Marc said, his voice slurring.

He looked groggy. "Are you all right?"

"I feel. I feel light. Airy."

"Shouldn't painkillers make you feel that way?"

"Never before."

Katrina picked up the orange bottle. "I gave you two as you asked." She looked closer. "Holy shit. I gave you Tyler's meds—Tylenol three and he only takes one."

Marc laughed. "That's why I'm feeling so—pain free. And happy. But drowsy. One is enough to knock out an elephant. Like Tyler. Tyler the elephant." He laughed, amused at his own inane joke.

She picked up another orange bottle and saw Marc's name. "Your medication has a tangerine lid. You should have said tangerine, not orange."

"Too late for oranges and tangerines. You've killed me for real, Katrina. Katrina Sherrerrrrr. Goodbye, my angry angel, my honey, my sweetie…," he sang.

Katrina dropped the pills and raced to him. "Oh my God. This isn't good. I didn't mean it, really." She raced to the door and banged on it. "Help!" She banged but the music was so loud, no one heard. She took out her phone, remembered the battery was drained, and threw it at the door. "I need your phone."

He put it under his leg, stretched out his arms, and puckered his lips.

Was he for real? Did the painkillers transport him back to teenage-hood? As much as she wanted a big smooch and more, she had to save him first. Otherwise, the lawsuit would be bigger than before. "Give me the damn phone now."

"Nope. You're yelling."

"I'm yelling because I have to call for help."

He pushed it higher, almost under his buttocks.

"You've got to be kidding me." She marched to him and stuck her hand under his seat. Marc threw her onto the bed and tickled her.

"There's no time for this, Marc." She rolled off the bed, landing on the carpet but with the prize in her hand.

Marc peered over the side. "You're no fun at all."

She jumped up. "I need to save you first." She moved as far away from him as possible and called Eric. He picked up after a long time. "Eric, it's Katrina. You have to help me. I gave Marc the wrong medication and double the dose, too. I gave him Tyler's Tylenol three. Ask Tyler. What the hell am I supposed to do? He's really—happy."

Eric spoke to Tyler and they laughed.

"Katrina, it's Tyler."

"Help, I've over drugged him."

"Get him into a shower and make him move around."

"But the shower will be cold."

"Even better."

"What about side effects or repercussions?"

"Extreme and utter nirvana." The phone went dead.

"Shit."

"You're swearing quite a bit, Katrina Sherrerrrrr." Marc wagged a finger and sang her name.

Gone was the charming king of the castle. In his place was an annoying adolescent prankster.

"I've only just begun." She threw the cell on the bed, grabbed two candles, and put them in the bathroom. "I have to get you into a shower."

"Will you join me?"

"No." Was he for real? "Now get up." With her arms around him, she helped him to the bathroom. She put down the toilet lid, pushed him onto it, and opened the shower head. It was lukewarm but soon it would be cold. "Okay, let's get you in."

"Only if you come in with me."

"I'll join you once you're in."

"You're lying."

"I promise."

"I'm holding you to it." He stood, swayed, and pulled his tie off. He was about to undo the buttons on his shirt but stopped. A sly smile curled his lips. He stretched out his arms and swayed toward her. "Help."

Katrina rolled her eyes. If she hadn't done this to him and she wasn't stuck in his room, she would charge out.

She began to unbutton his shirt, but seeing his

chest made her fingers fumble. He was the picture of a weightlifting, muscle crunching, cardio sweating-god only a professional athlete could be. The dusting of hair that crawled down his abs, into his pants, and, presumably, all the way down yonder where the puck and hockey stick had been strategically placed gave him away as a mere mortal.

Marc drew closer. "Are you afraid of me?" His voice was a sensuous whisper.

"Don't make me laugh."

"Then why are you going so slow?" More of the silky tone. "Rip my shirt off just like the movies."

She focused on the job or risked losing herself in his allure. "I can't afford to buy you another."

"I've got plenty. Come on. Rip it off. I work out. Me Tarzan. You Jane. Rip."

"This is not the jungle." She undid another button.

His eyes narrowed but glinted with slyness. "You *are* afraid of me."

Katrina yanked his shirt apart, buttons flying everywhere. "Satisfied?"

The shirt stuck over his rippled shoulder muscles. "You haven't finished."

She dragged it off, ripped it in half, and threw both pieces in his face. "Ripped."

Laughing, he batted them away.

Hands on her hips, she asked, "Any requests for the pants?"

His eyes lit. "With your teeth."

She turned. He pulled her back. "Just joking."

She undid his buckle and pulled his belt off.

Marc drew closer, his lips touching hers. "Unless you're up for it."

"I'm not."

He shrugged like a dejected little boy. "Another time, okay?"

"Absolutely not." She put her hands on his zipper but threw them right off.

"Alas, as you've so rightly noticed, it's a little crowded down there."

"Alas, I have rightly noticed." He was hard. He was aroused.

"All complements, of course."

"I'm flattered."

He waited and so did she. "You're up at bat, *honey*."

Keeping her gaze averted, she pulled his pants over his hips and down long and muscular, sculpture-perfect legs. The fine coat of hair on them tickled her hands. She fell on her haunches but hauled herself up on her knees. "Would you like to lift your feet, or do I bite them?"

"Now there's a thought."

"Lift your bloody feet and get in the shower."

"Both at the same time?"

Katrina held back her laughter. "One at a time, please."

He lifted one foot, then the other, and knocked his pants aside.

"Get in."

He looked at his boxers. "I still have clothes on."

Katrina couldn't. He was fully aroused. For her. The boxers were tight and left little to the imagination. How could she take them off and pretend at indifference when she did want to look at him, every glorious square inch?

"There's a surprise for you." He even winked.

"There's no surprise, Marc. I can see it."

He pulled his boxers to his ankles. "No, now you can see it." He took a step forward but stumbled sending her against the wall. He threw his arms around her to catch her. "Saved you."

"My hero." Katrina pushed him back and onto his feet. "Now step out of your boxers before you make any more sudden moves."

"Watch me." He kicked the boxers into the sink. "I'm a boxers Ninja."

As much as she didn't want to, Katrina burst into laughter. "Boxers Ninja Superhero." She indicated the shower. "Now get in, superhero."

He leaned against the door, folded his arms, and crossed his legs. He looked like he was waiting for the bus. But most men didn't wait naked and fully aroused at the bus stop. "No can do. It's your turn."

"I'm not the one who's high on medication and in need of cooling off."

"But you're the one who made me high on medication and in need of cooling off."

"And that's why I'm trying to help you, so get under the shower."

He shook his head several times. "You can't fool me, Katrina Sherrer, the meanest angel in the west."

"We're in the northeast."

He dramatically held onto the door for support. "I'm getting dizzier and dizzier and it's your fault."

"For someone who is supposedly drugged, you sound pretty clear—and you've watched far too many movies."

"Blame Great Aunt Hazel. She got me hooked on

all the classic movies. You want me to sing you some oldies? Her favorite was *Seven Brides for Seven Brothers*."

"I know the movie well."

"Hey, I'm stranded here in a snow storm too—with three of my hockey brothers." He leaned in closer. "You got three more sisters hidden away?"

"No, thankfully just the three obstinate ones out there."

"Too bad. I could have called up more of my hockey brothers. How did the song go, when the brothers go to the fair?"

"Why don't you think about it and sing it for me in the shower? Now get in."

He sat on the toilet and crossed his legs, but his erection was in the way. "No, first you take off your clothes."

Katrina laughed again, bringing a big smile to Marc's face.

"Fine." She took off her black workout jacket to reveal a black tank top.

"Was there a sale on black things?"

Katrina ignored him. "Okay, in you go."

"You gave me more medication than I needed but I can still see very well—better than very well, and sometimes two or three of you. You've got clothes on."

"I'm cold."

"I'll have you sweating in no time."

That was what she was afraid of.

She took off her runners and socks. "The pants come off when you're in the shower."

"I'll know if you don't take those pants off."

"I'm sure you will."

Kirsten Paul

With his gaze narrowed on her, Marc climbed into the shower as Katrina held him by the waist. Water poured over his rugged body and down his legs. A spasm of sheer want jolted through her. No man looked so good drenched in water. Damn. No man looked so good even without water. She thought the shower would cool him off, but he didn't mind, and his erection didn't suffer, either.

"It's nice and fresh in here. Now take all the black stuff off and get in. I promise you the best shower of your life—and maybe more if I convince you."

Katrina didn't need any convincing. That was the problem. "I have to make sure you don't fall."

He gripped the shower rod and leaned toward her. His chest expanded, the muscles rippling as water from his face dripped onto hers. "I won't fall, and I promise you won't fall either."

Katrina was both as taken aback as she was mesmerized.

Before she could move away, he pulled her in with all her clothes and planted her against him. She shouted not because the water was cold but because she slid into his wet body with incredible ease.

But it wasn't right, and she pushed him away. "It's bloody cold."

"Not for long." He pulled her back and kissed her, slipping his tongue between her lips. She went from cold to hot in an instant and forgot about everything. There was no inn, no debts, no creditors, and no worries about the future. He wasn't even the man who wanted to buy her inn. There was just him and her and wanting each other.

Marc pressed her against the tiles and pulled off

her tank top. "More black." He plucked at the straps of her bra. "Why are you wearing a sports bra? I hate sports bras. They're tight and rigid. Whoever designed them wasn't thinking about sex and ease."

He pulled at the bra when everything flooded back. Why couldn't she enjoy this moment with Marc and allow him to take off her bra?

She pushed him away and climbed out of the shower.

Because nothing would change between them or for her after they were together. It would be worse. She couldn't make love with the man who wanted to buy her property and kick her to the curb. Time for a reality check. There was no need for sex, no matter how much she wanted it. She had to just concentrate on working off the extra dose of Tylenol.

Water flowed down Marc's face, but she saw his confusion.

"I didn't make you warm?"

Katrina couldn't lie. "You made me very warm. But I need to make sure you get over the drugs first."

"Then we can try again?"

The cold water made her tremble. "Then you'll be thinking straighter, and I'll be thinking smarter."

"Is that a yes or a no?"

Why was he so lucid when he shouldn't be? "No." But did she ever want to say yes. She wanted to scream it.

Marc shook his head. "That's what I get for finding an angel. All practical and business and she's even wearing an ugly sports bra. It interrupts all the flow of passion."

All hail the sports bra, Katrina thought as she held

a towel open for him. Marc stepped out and she draped it around him.

"You're shivering, Katrina." He grabbed another towel, whipped it around her, and dried her. "You need to take those clothes off. They're wet."

"I will." She could barely talk she was so cold. But he had unraveled her. She'd shiver until she could be rough and tough again. "Once I get you settled."

He leaned against the sink, the towel around his shoulders, and folded his arms. "I'm settled."

Without offering any resistance, Katrina removed her yoga pants. She stood in a wet bra and panties.

Marc took her all in, his head shaking. "I should have known. More black and more practicality." He sat on the toilet, pulled her toward him, and slid his fingers through the legs of her boy shorts. "Sports undies."

Katrina shivered but moaned in pleasure. She couldn't stop herself.

"I hate sports undies. No sex to them. Do you do yoga?" His breath was warm against her skin.

"Once upon a time."

"Too bad. All the meditation would make it easier for you to bend to my will if you still did."

But his hands went slack, and his head drooped against her belly.

"Marc?"

Nothing.

The drugs!

"Marc?"

He jumped up, his head hitting her jaw. "What happened?"

She massaged her jaw. "You can't sleep."

"Me, sleep on you?" His head drooped again,

landing on her shoulder. He kissed her neck. "Never."

The little kiss melted her. She pushed him away, but he didn't budge. "Sing me a song, Marc. Do you remember the song from *Seven Brides for Seven Brothers*? Or can you sing me some other oldie?"

Marc reared his head and thought about it for a long minute. "*Ev'ry morning, ev'ry evening, ain't we got fun. Not much money, oh but honey, ain't we got fun. The rents unpaid dear, we haven't a bus...*"

Katrina was relieved. She couldn't let him fall asleep. She pushed him onto the toilet. "Keep going, Marc."

While he sang she held the towel with one hand, removed her wet bra and panties with the other and wrapped the towel around herself. He watched her every move and went off key many times, but he was enthusiastic and even winked. More important, it kept him awake.

"Hey, we match." He indicated the towels.

"We do. Let's go near the fireplace."

"Oh, you want to make love on the bear rug, don't you? You've watched a lot of old films like Great Aunt Hazel and me, too."

"There's no bear rug. We're walking around the fireplace."

"But what about the movies? And my foot?"

"Marc, I almost killed you out there in the blizzard and now I'm about to kill you again. I can't afford your death on my conscience. It's too overloaded already. We're walking. Sore foot or not." She hauled him up and slung her arm around his waist.

He draped his arm around her shoulder. "Do you want me to sing while I walk through the agony of my ankle?"

"Yes, it would be lovely."

"Come on and hear, come on and hear Alexander's ragtime band. Come and hear, come on and hear, it's the best band in the land..."

Someone knocked at the door. "Marc?" It was Tyler.

"No Marc here. It's Mr. January Hockey Player."

"Mr. January Hockey Player? What happened to Marc?"

"Ask Katrina. She doesn't want to see him or the CEO of King Court Development—the name of my company, right? So I covered him up with Mr. January Hockey Player." He laughed at himself. "I'm not really covered up, am I?"

Oh, he was in nirvana all right. "I never said I didn't like you," Katrina said.

"Then you're fooling me. You don't like me—Marc and Mr. CEO because they want to buy you out, so I'll only speak as Mr. January Hockey Player. He's hanging in your office, telling you what day it is. He's nice and quiet—submissive, too," he added with a big grin.

"Are you in trouble, Mr. January Hockey Player?" Tyler asked.

"He's gloriously high," Katrina said.

"I am not high. I'm having the time of my life. Katrina and I are walking around with not much on and I'm serenading her."

"You're right, Katrina," Tyler said. "He's gloriously high but happy. Maybe I should take an extra dose next time and feel as good as him."

"No time to speak to you, Tyler. Have to sing. *By*

the light of the silvery moon…"

"How long before the meds wear off?" Katrina shouted over Marc's singing.

"Soon," Tyler said. "Just keep him active. Can you play hockey?"

"Hockey?" Marc said with glee. "Score on me, Katrina. I'm a defenseman but I'll let you score on me. Just don't tell the coach."

"No playing hockey inside, Marc."

Marc was disappointed. "Can I make a better suggestion?"

"No." She flatly said it. She wasn't sleeping with the enemy.

"You can tie me up and I'll be submissive. You wanted me to bend to your wishes before. I'll do it now. Wholeheartedly," he sang.

"No."

"Just tie me up, then?"

"No."

"Wow, he is high," Tyler said, laughing. "Have a good evening, Katrina. You too—Mr. January Hockey Player."

"Tyler?" Katrina called.

"I'm still here."

"I made dough for egg bread. It's on the shelf over the stove. Can you or one of my sisters put it in the fridge for me, please?"

"You are such a caring chef, Katrina," Marc said, "thinking about your poor egg dough on the shelf."

"Not a problem," Tyler said.

Music blared again from the lobby.

Marc threw her away from him but held onto her hand. "Let's dance."

"I thought your ankle hurt."

"I lied. It feels good. Actually, I can't feel it." He pulled her into his arms and out again, swung her, dipped her, twirled her, stamped his feet, and clapped his hands around her and either hummed or sang lyrics to songs.

"You're a pretty good dancer," Katrina said with a laugh. "Better than a singer. Did Great Aunt Hazel teach you?"

"No, my grandmother. She was a professional dancer and still rumbas and waltzes. She looked after my brother and me when we were young and insisted we learn. She said it would always guarantee us a lovely lady."

His grandmother was right. She was ready to go to the wrong side with Marc. But she was ready even before the dancing began.

"You should meet her and Great Aunt Hazel. Do you want to talk to them? Where's my cell?"

"No, no, they both sound like lovely ladies, but they're probably sleeping now."

"You're right. I'm getting tired, too, Katrina."

"You can't sleep until the drugs wear off."

"Then we need to take the dance down many tempos." He tucked her in his arms, nestling her head under his chin and they did a very long and slow dance while Marc hummed away. She felt him fall asleep a few times and each time nudged him awake. But it was difficult to continue. She wanted to sleep, too, in his warm arms and against his beating heart.

An hour later, exhausted from dancing and walking and shouting at Marc to stay awake, Katrina tucked him into bed under several blankets. Marc mumbled something. He drew her head down and kissed her. It was a sweet and honest kiss. The kind of kiss a man gave the woman in his life when he wanted to simply and succinctly tell her he loved and respected her. That he cherished her and was thankful.

The kiss disarmed her more than the kiss in the shower and brought tears to Katrina's eyes. As much as she wanted the hot and heavy and sweaty lovemaking, the one little tender kiss made her realize how alone and lonely she was, and how much she didn't want to be.

She fell into the wing chair near the bed, exhausted beyond words, pulled up her legs, and cocooned herself in a blanket.

How could a man she swore she hated, arouse such a mishmash of emotion and longing in her, and in such a short time?

Chapter Nine

Katrina was freezing. Why was she so cold?

She shuffled but something banged against her ribs. She pried her eyes open. She was in a wing chair and in total darkness.

She jumped up. She fell asleep in the chair next to Marc's bed.

Marc!

She leaped forward. Marc was on his side, facing her.

Was he dead? Did she kill him for real with the two doses of Tylenol three?

He shuffled.

He wasn't dead. Thank goodness. He slept soundly, very peacefully actually, with the blankets and duvet up to his chin.

Katrina moved back into the chair. She was cold. She was wrapped in only a towel and a light blanket and the fire was out. Except for a couple candles, all the others were burned to the end.

She padded to the fireplace, the hardwood floor feeling like an ice rink under her feet and moved the embers around. There were a couple sparks but nothing else. She had no more wood either. The room would get colder and colder. She tried the door, but the power was still out, too. It was quiet in the lobby. Her sisters and the guys were probably sleeping.

She was freezing. She grabbed her clothes from the bathroom floor, but they were still wet and icy cold, too. She couldn't put them on and dropped them.

She spied Marc's clothes. His jacket lay on the foot of the bed, his pants near the bathroom door, his shirt at the foot of the tub, and his boxers were draped on the sink. She picked up the pants. They were dry.

She grabbed everything except the boxers, including the ripped shirt. They were all dry, but then he didn't go into the shower with them.

Marc didn't need them. She did.

She slid both halves of the shirt over each arm and brought them together over her breasts. The shirt was big and fell below her hips. Most of the buttons had popped out, too, but she didn't care.

The scent of a soft cologne wafted around her. She held the sleeve to her nose. She didn't know what cologne it was, but it smelled wonderful. Of vigor, vitality, and masculinity. Of strength and seduction. It was Marc and a spasm of want coursed through her body again.

She had to get over him. This longing and wanting for the man who wanted to put her out on the street would not do.

She pulled on his pants, twined the shirt around herself, drew the pants over her breasts, tied them together with his belt, and topped everything with the jacket. Armani. It was the closest she'd get to a designer outfit. Armani or not, she didn't need anyone to tell her she looked like Charlie Chaplin minus the bowler hat.

She scooped up her clothes and draped them near the dying embers of the fireplace. Her hair was damp.

She loosened the elastic and her curls tumbled below her shoulders in a wild mess. She couldn't do anything with her hair. Not that she needed to. She wasn't about to seduce Marc. She glanced at him. Even though it was intolerably tempting.

She moved around to get warm, almost tripping on the bottom of his pants. Marc looked warm and comfortable in the bed. Very warm, in fact, snuggled deeply under the blankets. The bed and blankets invited her.

Who was she kidding? Marc in the bed and under the blankets invited her.

But she couldn't. He was a guest and her sworn enemy.

She ambled to the window and pulled the drapes apart. The wind and sleet had stopped but snow still fell heavily. It reached just below the window.

She shivered. Shit. Even with the suit on, she was cold.

Marc moaned. He wasn't cold.

She raced to the bed and without taking off Marc's clothes, crawled under the blankets next to him. Marc stirred, turned, and put his arm around her as though it was the most natural thing to do.

Katrina wondered who he thought she was, but she didn't care. It was nice, and she was warm.

She adjusted herself more comfortably and watched him sleep.

He was gorgeous. Johansen was a Scandinavian name. From Norway or Denmark or possibly Sweden, depending on how he spelt it. He looked like he came from strong Nordic roots. Tall, fair-skinned, wavy dark blond hair, and light blue eyes all screamed Nordic ancestors. But he was born and raised in King Court. Just like she had.

She rubbed her nose against his hair. It had gotten wet in the shower but dried while they danced. It was crisp but soft at the same time.

She wanted to kiss him without reservation or anger or fear. With a clear mind and a happy heart.

She would start with his lips, the lower one, the upper, both together, move above them, slide to his cheeks, glide up to his eyes, skim over to his ears and return to his lips, where she would tease them, slip her tongue inside, and revel in the heat and balm of his mouth.

"Katrina?"

She gasped and leaped from the bed, but he held her. "I'm sorry if I woke you but I'm freezing."

He tucked the blankets over her shoulders and curled his leg over hers. "You're lumpy."

"I'm wearing clothes. Your clothes."

"All of them?"

"Pants, shirt, belt, and jacket. No tie or boxers."

His laugh was soft, the warmth of his breath cool but warm against her cheek. "You forgot about my socks and shoes."

"I couldn't find them."

"We kicked them under the bed while we danced."

"You remember?"

"I remember. I apologize if I did or said anything improper."

Katrina laughed. "It was all improper but entertaining. No harm done. How are you feeling?"

"My foot's a little sore but I'm good. I feel very rested, like I had a good sleep."

"I think you did. Any dizziness or headache?"

"You sound like a doctor."

Katrina grimaced. "I'm sorry about the pill mix up."

"No harm done. I'll remember to say tangerine instead of orange next time." He moved her closer. "Do you need all those clothes? I can keep you warmer."

Katrina got hotter. "That's what I'm afraid of."

He kissed her. She was lying down but swooned.

"Take everything off, Katrina, or I will." Again, the beautiful sensuous whisper. This time she would give in. She knew she shouldn't. She knew she should get out of the bed and go sit by herself in the wing chair again. But she didn't want to. She wanted to stay next to Marc. She wanted to remove her clothes and feel the heat of his body against the cold of hers.

She slipped out of the bed and took off his jacket and pants. She stood in his torn shirt, wondering if she really should peel it off.

"Allow me." He threw the blankets off. She had wrapped a dry towel around him before helping him into bed, but he had nothing on now.

He moved to the edge of the bed, enveloped her with his legs, and kissed her between the breasts. He parted the shirt and nuzzled her breasts. "You've saved me the trouble of pulling your ugly bra off."

Katrina moved herself deeper between his legs, until she felt his erection against her belly. She slipped her hands through his hair. "It was still wet."

He cupped her breasts, sending spasms of heat through her. "You're more beautiful without it."

She slid her hand from his hair down his cheek and traced his lips. "I look a mess."

He stood up, standing a head taller than her, and framed her face with his hands. "I have never seen a more beautiful mess in my life."

Katrina laughed against his chest.

"Now for the rules."

Katrina gazed at him. "You have rules?"

"Only for you. You're too uptight and upstanding and they're only for tonight. For tonight, I'm just Marc and you're just Katrina. There is nothing between us. No anger, no hatred, no pain, no defenses, no inn or restaurant, and definitely no *ego*. Nothing."

Katrina couldn't even remember why she had to forget about anger and pain and defenses and the inn and restaurant and whatever else he said and made one little nod.

His hands moved into her hair. "I want you and you want me and nothing else in between." He brushed her lips. "No pulling away from me."

Katrina kissed him. "Marc?"

"Yes?"

"Before I remember everything I'm not supposed to, can we get started?"

Marc laughed, his breath tickling her neck. He peeled the shirt off and laughed again when it ripped in two. He flipped her onto the bed and moved on top.

She pulled his face down and kissed him without anger, hatred, pain, or defenses. She wanted to be with him. She wanted his body around her and nothing else.

They were half on and half off the bed. Marc raised himself and pulled her higher until her head was on the pillow. "How do you want me, Katrina?"

"You're giving me free rein?"

"You like to be the boss."

Laughing, she raised her chest, offering him her breasts. He took one nipple in his mouth and sucked it until she felt a delirious tightness stemming from her crotch through to her entire body. She moaned long and in satisfaction. "I want to see you, Marc."

Marc rolled onto the bed and pulled her on top. Katrina straddled him, her legs lightly winding around his hips. He held her up with his knees.

Her hands flowed down his thick thighs as he caressed her hips.

"You may be a strong woman, but your body looks like I could snap it in two."

Katrina's smile was sly. "You won't. I can take you on."

"Oh, I know you can. I've known you could since you wiped my blood from my face out in the blizzard." He pulled her by the hips over his head. "I want to give you this."

She couldn't speak and nodded. She rose on her knees and he tasted her. As she held onto the headboard, he stroked her with a rhythmic hunger. Katrina's body tightened in sheer delight.

It had been so long since she felt so tight and so free. Like a woman and not a workhorse.

"I'm ready for you, Marc," she murmured.

He gripped her and thrust his tongue inside her. Katrina didn't need more. She let out a deep moan of ecstasy, her body breaking into glorious spasms of release.

But he kept on going. He wanted her to break again and she did, this time with a silent cry of joy.

Marc flipped her onto her back. She folded her legs around his hips afraid if she let him go, she would be without support and flung her hands against the headboard. But he loosened himself and inserted his fingers inside her. "You're ready for me, my love."

My love? She couldn't remember ever being called my love, whether in the heat of lovemaking or not. Even by the one man who once professed to love her.

Katrina nodded, unable to say anything.

He pulled his fingers out and slipped in, sliding and pushing deeper and harder. "Hold me, Katrina."

Katrina let go of the headboard and twinned her fingers through his.

"Look at me."

She opened her eyes. Except for the few flickering candles, it was dark, but she saw him. He was even more beautiful in the heat of desire.

But he pulled himself out.

Katrina gasped, wanting to cry.

"Are you protected?" His words came out on a breath.

"Yes," she all but screamed. "Yes."

Marc pushed himself back in and thrust. Katrina wrapped her legs around his back until he groaned, thrust again and again and fell on top of her.

She stroked his back as he came down from his high. A film of sweat was on his body or hers. She didn't know and didn't care. It was communal. It was shared, and she wanted to cry.

If lovemaking was so beautiful hating him, how would it feel loving him?

Chapter Ten

Marc went up on an elbow. He wanted to see Katrina's face. Even with the dying light from the candles, he saw she was flushed from lovemaking.

Katrina looked even more beautiful now. Ethereal. Her blue eyes were clear and tranquil, and no anxiety flashed in them.

He pushed her curls off her cheeks, tucking them behind her ears. He made her look like that. He brought on her quiet satisfaction and serenity. The dusty red of her lips was his doing, too. It pleased him, and he didn't want anyone else touching her. Just him. But it was simply wish fulfilment. He didn't know how he melted Katrina's defenses and got her to be with him.

But he wanted her again. Once was not enough. He also wanted more to go with it. To see her beyond tonight and to know everything about her.

The realization surprised and excited him.

"So, do you still hate me?" he asked.

Katrina's smile was unexpectedly sly. "Do you still want to buy my inn and land and not bend to my will?"

He caressed her soft form to the hard contours of his legs and chest. "Yes."

"Then I still have to hate you."

"So, you really don't hate me, then?"

She snuggled against him, smiling when she felt him get hard again. "I have to."

"Have to is not the same as actually hating me."

"It is necessary for me to hate you."

"But not the truth."

Katrina rolled onto her side and laughed. It was one of the few times he heard her laugh with joy, and it was the softest and most musical sound he heard.

"Hey, no turning your back on me. I'll do whatever it takes to make you look at me again, including downing two more of those Tylenol three tablets."

She faced him and placed her hand on his cheek. "You don't have to do anything to get me to look at you again, Marc. I can't stop myself. That's been the problem."

"Well, I'm glad you have this problem." He kissed her lips, nose, eyes, cheeks, and jaw until she became soft and pliable again.

"But nothing has changed," she whispered, kissing his ears. She pressed her hand against his chest to hold him back. "I will have to sign those papers and turn everything over to you. And everything my family has known for over a hundred and fifty years will be no more. It will all be gone. My parents will retire in Florida, my sisters will move onto their own lives and me. I don't know where I'll be, but it certainly won't be here."

"There's a lot out there for a talented woman like you."

"You mean like basting ribs?"

"Don't put yourself down. You'll find the right place."

"My place was always supposed to be here. It's hard to rethink it—and myself."

"You don't have to be alone while you're

103

rethinking yourself. You can be with me."

Katrina pulled her head back. "You weren't talking crazy when you were on the Tylenols but now without them in your system you are."

He was taken aback. Was he the only one to feel there could be more between them than one night of sex? "Why am I crazy?"

"Because we were thrown together. It's just one night—actually just a moment. Once the god of electricity gets his or her act together and opens the door, we're back to the way we were before it closed us in. You'll go on to your hockey and commercials and multi-millions and a whole lot of beautiful woman who wear perfect makeup and expensive clothes—and no ugly black sports bras when they're with you. Women who won't try and kill you with Tylenol three tablets and tell you they hate you."

"Is that who you think I am?"

"Isn't it?"

He shrugged. "Yes."

Katrina pushed him away. "You really do have such an ego. More than I ever had."

Marc laughed as he pulled her back. "Occupational hazard."

"That's probably the only thing we can agree on. At least you're honest."

"And so are you." He stroked and smoothed her body until it melted against his. "What's wrong with wanting to be with one woman who isn't afraid not to wear makeup or ugly black sports bras, which still, by the way, looked wonderful on her, or tell me what she hates about me. I'm going to assume the Tylenol three was a mistake and not a planned assassination."

Her eyes rounded. "Has your ego even suffered or your conscience squirmed since I told you what I think about you?"

"Nope. I know where you stand. I know who you are, and I know who I am."

Katrina's lips parted as though she wanted to say something, but nothing came out.

"You're all bare to me. Gloriously and sinfully and beautifully bare." He stroked her cheek. "No makeup masking your face and eyes." He slid his hand into her hair. "No tight arrangement manipulating your hair." He traced her lips. "Nothing but the truth from you. It's not something I come across very often—if at all."

Katrina was silent for a long time. He could see her eyes dancing, searching for the right words. "I'm a mess, Marc, and I really haven't been hospitable to you. I've—put up with you."

"Yes," he laughed. "But you're better than hospitable. You're honest and yourself. You're a mess I want to get to know. I don't mind being with you as you *un-mess* yourself."

She shook her head. "You're crazy. Once the door opens, I'm leaving."

"Fine, but I've told you why it doesn't have to happen. Now, why don't you tell me why you still have to leave?"

"Because I have to hate you."

"Of course, I forgot." She grabbed at feeble answers and it pleased him. "But what if you didn't have to hate me? Would you leave then?"

She pulled her lips to one side and considered the question. "You're a guest and I'm the innkeeper. It's not right, so, yes, I have to leave."

"Ah, but officially I'm not a guest. I dropped in unannounced, and I never registered or paid for my room."

Katrina took a deep breath. He saw the wheels of her thoughts turning in her eyes as she prepared for some other feeble excuse. "Still won't work. Your name starts with the same letter as my last boyfriend. Actually, the first three letters of your name are the exact same. He was a complete asshole, so, yes, I do have to leave."

"Now, that is very interesting. M. A. R. Is it Mark with a k instead of a c?" Katrina shook her head. "Marino. It's Marino, right, an Italian soccer player who plays for the national team." Another shake of her head. "Marius, a Swedish Olympic skier?" She shook her head again. "I know, Markus from Russia. Markus the spy."

"Martin from London, Ontario."

"Martin from London, Ontario was an asshole. I'm glad you dumped him."

"He dumped me."

Marc pulled back in disbelief.

"He thought I was rich."

"Martin was more than an asshole. He was scum. But his loss is my gain. I want you just the way you are."

Katrina's smile fell. "No, you don't. I'm not nice anymore." She threw the blankets off and sat up. But shivering, she tossed them back on and curled against him. "Shit, if it wasn't so cold and I wasn't stuck in here, I would leave."

Marc pulled her against him. "Do you have to be nice?"

"No, but I liked myself better when I was. When I was nice, and I didn't make a mess of the inn. When I had an ego, too, and I knew where I was going. I'm all over the place now and will be again when the god of electricity opens the door and lets me out of this room. And I certainly will be when I sign those papers selling you the inn and property."

"So I'll be with you until all the pieces come back together again."

Katrina looked at him for a very long time. "Marc, no matter how you look at it, you're the guy who will buy up everything I can't bring myself to sell and the guy who will tear down everything I know and want. Do you really think I can put all that aside and jump into an honest-to-goodness relationship with you?"

Marc thought about it for a long time. "Yes."

Katrina laughed. "You're mad."

"Yes, mad about you."

"Stop the flattery. I hate flattery. It's so empty."

Marc flinched. "I'm not flattering you. I may be many things you don't like but I'm not flattering you. I don't need to flatter to get what I want. I want you in my life. It's the honest truth."

Katrina was silent. "But you're still the bad guy."

"I'm the bad guy because you see me as one."

Katrina didn't seem to know what to say. "There's no winning with you."

"You're right. You should have scored on me when you had the chance."

She took a deep breath. "I should check the door." She threw off the blankets, put on his jacket, and shivering, strode to it. "The power may have come back. It's time to remember everything and leave."

Marc waited. Was he nervous? He was, and it surprised him.

Katrina turned the knob and the door clicked open.

Marc jumped out of the bed. Was she leaving? It felt more like she was leaving him and not the room and their situation.

"Katrina?" His voice was a plea. He had never pleaded for a woman to stay with him. It felt worse than an illegal crosscheck by some two-hundred-fifty-pound defenseman.

Katrina held the door open. A candle flickered on the wash stand next to her. He saw her determination to keep a stone-cold face and leave. But sadness crept into her eyes

She closed the door and locked it.

Marc sighed in relief.

"I don't believe I'm doing this." She threw off the jacket and strode to the bed.

Marc wrapped himself around her. "Are you back because it's cold?"

Katrina shook her head against his shoulder. "Can we go back to those rules you set out before we began? Can we leave things the way they are for tonight? I'm here with you now because I want to be, but tomorrow I'm back to me. Beyond signing those papers, I'm nowhere near to making any other decision or promise."

"Fair enough." He kissed her as though he never would again. He didn't like her terms but for now they would do. He'd work on it, on her. He'd make her believe she could sell, be with him, and have hope for her future.

It was cold without the blankets, but he threw them

off and trailed kisses down her body until she writhed with desire again.

Katrina came as he held her. She was about to take him in her mouth, but he could wait. "Can I suggest something, Katrina? About the inn?"

"I'm at the end of hopelessness with the inn. Shoot. I have nothing to lose."

"I'm sure I'll be snowed in until the roads are cleared, and I can arrange for transportation out of here."

"It usually takes a day or two for snow plows to reach us."

"Good. Then show me your property—all of it. It was your original plan when you asked me to visit. Sell me on your idea for the inn and then I'll decide whether to consider it or to turn the property and inn into a residential development."

Katrina's eyes rounded with hope. "You'll really go out there, see all of it, and listen to my ideas?"

"Yes, to all your ideas. You tell me everything you would like to do with the inn and property if you had the chance. Don't keep anything back and then I'll make my decision. I'm not saying I will reconsider buying. I will buy, but I will listen to your proposal and decide if it has merit."

"And you're going to do this because the god of electricity put me in bed with you?"

"I'm going to do this because the god of electricity gave me a chance with you and I want the chance to continue. I'm going to do this because the sooner you're not in pieces and hopeful, and you believe in my sincerity, the better for me."

Katrina's kiss was gentle but filled with what he

was sure was the beginnings of love.

"You have a deal, Mr. Johansen."

That was all he wanted. He gave her hope again. It could be short-lived, but it offered him the chance to win her over.

Marc threw his leg over hers. "In the meantime, Ms. Sherrer, shall we rumba, waltz or tango?"

"All of them, Mr. Johansen. Absolutely, all of them."

Chapter Eleven

Katrina stirred. At once both hot and cold. She tried to turn onto her side, but she was locked in Marc's arms. Securely.

She snuggled into him, not wanting to leave. The lovemaking was wonderful. The first time in a heated encounter of sheer want and desire. The second time slowly and leisurely. They laughed. She couldn't remember ever laughing during lovemaking with any of her former partners. She couldn't remember the last time she laughed, *period.* That was wonderful in itself. She didn't realize until then how much she longed for a time, however fleeting, where she didn't have any worries or fears in her life. When she wasn't alone.

Her moment with Marc was unexpected, different, and one she would always cherish. Marc was different. He wasn't the cold-blooded businessman she expected of the CEO of King Court Development. He had a heart and it pierced through her hard shell, reminding her she had one too. That was the problem. It made hating him so much harder, now.

But their brief time together was over. Marc spoke about continuing but she knew better. He was only here to get her to sign those papers. The night together was a slip and a diversion. He would forget about her the instant he left the inn, possibly when she signed the papers giving him ownership of the land. She wasn't about to delude herself. A man with everything and who was somebody didn't want to get involved with a woman with nothing. A woman who was a nobody and made such a mess of her family's livelihood and her own. He could rob her of her livelihood and history, but he would not rob her of the only thing left. Her pride. She needed to hold onto some of it.

They were over, and she was back in the real world. She had to get breakfast going, probably lunch and dinner, too, clean up whatever disaster her sisters, Eric, Tyler, and Jakob made, clean their rooms, and then take the snow plows and dig the inn out. But she looked forward to showing Marc the entire property.

Maybe there was a way to salvage the inn and give her father hope again. To give *her* hope, too. She would even sell as long as the inn stayed true to its original design but with the necessary additions to bring it into the twenty-first century and make it competitive again. Then, maybe, she could stay on, keep the restaurant going the way she envisioned it, and finally get a star or two or better yet, a three-star rating. She knew she could get it. She was better than good. She was an exceptional chef. It was all she wanted. She'd be happy even if it wasn't her own restaurant. Not really, but she'd make do. She'd feel better about herself and maybe even consider being with a man like Marc.

But enough of dreams, especially her own. They got her and her family into trouble and she couldn't let them get in the way again. She would do her best to get Marc to see the viability of her vision. If she couldn't, then her last shot at hope was blown. She would lose the inn and restaurant to the very man heating her body. To the man who warmed her heart and reminded her of the possibility of hope and love. The world would then officially know. Katrina Sherrer's selfish dreams ruined her family.

She got up before she wallowed in self-pity. But before she did anything, she'd call her mother and see how her father was.

Careful not to upset Marc, she rolled onto her back. Marc grumbled but moved onto his side, his back to her. Katrina slipped out, wrapped the towel around herself, grabbed her clothes, and padded to the door. The knob clicked open and she slipped into the hall.

Marc's room was cold, but the hall was colder. It felt like she was walking through a freezer. She should have reset the thermostat during the night, when the power came back on, but her thoughts were only about Marc. She hoped her sisters wouldn't see her coming out of his room, wrapped in a towel. They'd never let her forget it and she needed to.

She stopped short in the lobby. The fire was burned out in the fireplace and everybody was sprawled out somewhere, fast asleep. Rebeka had put together two wing chairs and slept under a pile of blankets. Eric sat in another wing chair, half off, half on with blankets falling off. Ingrid and Tyler were on the floor, their backs to each other, near the fireplace wrapped in coats and blankets. Annelise was on the sofa, barely visible under a load of blankets with Jakob on the floor beside her, rolled into a duvet. They held hands.

It was so sweet. Nothing happened between them. Nothing looked like it happened between the others either. Empty wine bottles littered the floor, along with dirty plates, but they respected her father's rule. No sex under the roof of the inn.

Except her. She broke her father's rule. She who never broke any rule. But then, if she didn't convince Marc to keep the inn intact and simply add in the necessities, it wouldn't matter anymore. The inn would belong to him. There would be no roof to the inn and no rules to obey but many roofs, housing many families with their own rules.

She tiptoed behind the front desk and reset the thermostat. The furnace jolted into life. The lobby and kitchen would be warm when everyone woke up.

She raced through the kitchen toward the family's quarters. She remembered the dough for egg bread in the fridge and removed it. She set it on the counter and moved off to her bedroom. It was a disaster. Her bed was unmade and had been for as long as she could remember. Clothes and books and food magazines were thrown everywhere. She was too busy keeping the inn running to bother about her room.

Marc would laugh if he saw it. He wouldn't believe it was hers.

Katrina had to get Marc off her mind. Thinking and dreaming about him wouldn't put breakfast on the table or clear the snow or convince him of the viability of her ideas for the inn.

She plugged in her cell and took a quick shower. The water was cool, but she needed to wake up and start on what would be a very long and exhausting day.

Surprisingly, tears sprang into her eyes. Why was she about to cry? She had never cried before about all the work she did in the inn.

Did Marc do that to her? Did he remind her she was flesh and blood and not a machine? Or was it because she had one last chance to save the inn and possibly help her father get better? She held her face up to the water to wash the tears away. Whatever it was, she had no time to think about the reason. It would not change the outcome or lessen her work. Time to set her emotions aside and do what needed to be done.

She washed her hair, dried herself, and looked for clean clothes. She was about to put on another pair of black yoga pants but stopped. Too much black, Marc said.

Well, so what? She pulled them on.

Shit. She pulled them right back off again. Damn the man. He was even making her think about her scarce wardrobe. She looked around for something clean and not black. Nothing. Absolutely nothing. Black yoga pants or black jeans along with a black top and matching hoodie. Those were the only clean things.

There was no choice. She pulled on the top and hoodie and decided on the jeans. She thought about blow drying her hair, but it would take too long and only become unrulier. She would let it air dry. By the time Marc—forget Marc—by the time everyone woke up, her hair would be dry and tied back in a practical ponytail.

Her phone battery was at a good level. She sent her mother a text. "How's Dad? Please call." She put it in her hoodie's pocket and returned to the lobby. She added some wood to the fireplace and it flared up. Along with the furnace the lobby would be nicely heated by the time everyone woke up. It was only Marc's room she couldn't heat up. She could, but it would mean taking some logs there and starting the fireplace up. She couldn't risk the chance of ending up in his warm bed again. Marc's room needed to remain cold.

She parted the shutters of the lobby windows. The storm was over. A beautiful winter wonderland of pure white snow and ice, glistening like crystal on the trees and bushes stared back at her. The only problem with the winter wonderland was someone needed to plow all the beautiful white stuff to ensure they got out and others got in. That someone was her. Her sisters might shovel but they left the heavy tasks to her.

She was about to go into the kitchen when she remembered the condoms under the napkin. All of them were still there. Well, at least her sisters couldn't accuse her of being prudish. She had prepared them for the eventually.

She threw them back in the drawer of the front desk. Her sisters' time for carnal pleasures had come and gone.

In the kitchen, she tied her hair in a low ponytail, put on an apron, rolled out the dough, and made three loaves. She left them on the counter under a towel to proof and checked the fridge and freezer. The food was still cold. Nothing went bad with the power outage.

Time to make breakfast for her guests. They'd all be waking up sooner or later and be hungry.

But first her. She made herself a double espresso. While drinking it, she cut up potatoes, red peppers, and onions, added some seasoning and oil, and stuck them in the oven to bake. She removed homemade sausages from the freezer, thawed them, and put them in the oven, too. She prepared eggs for omelets and set them aside. The bread had doubled while resting on the stove. All three loaves went in the oven. It wouldn't be long before the kitchen smelled wonderful and brought in someone who wasn't snoozing anymore.

But what about lunch and dinner? Possibly lamb burgers and sweet potato fries for lunch and tourtière for dinner. She removed the ingredients when Jakob walked in, wearing his coat, gloves, scarf, hat, and a duvet over his shoulders.

"Good morning." He pulled off the duvet and threw it on a chair. "It's nice and warm in here and it smells wonderful. I assume the power came back on?"

She opened a container of Greek yogurt and put some in a bowl. Her breakfast. "It did. Breakfast should be ready soon. Would you like some coffee?"

"Love some."

"Is a mushroom and goat cheese omelet okay with you?"

"Any omelet would be good for me. I'm always hungry and from what I ate last night, anything you cook is wonderful. Can I help you with something?"

She put some berries, kiwis, and bananas in a bowl and set it on the table. "You can turn on the coffee maker."

He flicked it on and sat at the table. When the kitchen bustled with chefs and servers, they ate their meals and had meetings at the table. When it wasn't, the family ate their meals there. It was strange to see a guest sitting at the table.

"You don't want to sit in the dining room?" She indicated the white kitchen swing doors, leading to the restaurant. Her throat constricted with emotion. It had been over a month since anyone ate there.

"No, it smells delicious in here. I don't cook much for myself and miss the smell of food cooking in my family's kitchen."

Annelise walked in, wrapped in her coat and a blanket. "Good morning."

Jakob got up and kissed her. He remembered Katrina and meekly sat down.

"Nothing happened last night." Annelise's tone was abrasive.

Jakob's face went red. "I understood where you were coming from, Katrina. My parents have the same rule even though my brothers often broke it."

Katrina smiled. He was a good boy and he and Annelise were smitten. Their honesty and respect deserved more than a regular coffee. "Would you prefer a *café au lait*?"

"I would love one."

"Me, too?" Annelise asked.

"You too." She moved to the espresso machine.

"Do you want me to set the table?"

Wow, she was smitten. She'd never asked before. Love was certainly in the air.

She froze. Love did not happen overnight. And it certainly wouldn't happen to her or Marc. It was one night, a moment, and nothing more. There was too much between them. No matter how much she thought about him or all his talk about wanting to be with her.

"It would be nice," she mumbled.

"I'll help," Jakob said. They set the table for eight people and laughed about small things. Big or small knives? Large or small plates? Folded napkins or not? Done together, everything was exciting. When they finished, Katrina handed them their cups of *café au lait*. She pulled the sausages, potatoes, and bread out of the oven and let them settle while Jakob and Annelise sipped at their coffee. They returned the blanket and duvet to the lobby and snuggled against each other by the window, extending the length of a wall and laughed about the snow.

How sweet and uncomplicated. She had felt the same way once with what was his name in grade ten? She prepared their omelets and tried to remember. Damn, what was the guy's name? She should remember. He was her first boyfriend. She remembered every man's name since whatever-his-name-was in grade ten, but did it matter? He held no significance for her. Marc stood so far above him, above every other man who followed, too. He even made her want to forgive Martin's betrayal.

She almost dropped an omelet on the floor as she slid it onto a plate. She had to turn Marc into one of those men in her past. She was with the man one night. She was not a teenager like Annelise and Jakob, where anything and everything was possible, including love at first sight. Love could not happen to her in one night. She knew better.

"Breakfast is ready." Katrina set the potatoes, sausages, and egg bread on the table and put a plate with an omelet for both Jakob and Annelise on their place settings. They rushed over and helped themselves.

Jakob was on his second piece of everything when Marc came into the kitchen, walking easier on his bruised foot. He had his suit on and his shirt didn't even look ripped even though most of the buttons were missing. His tie was draped loosely over the shirt, hiding the lack of buttons, but the hairs of his chest peeked out. His hair was damp and except for the stubble around his chin and the bandage over his eye, he looked rested and composed.

"Good morning." His gaze rested on Katrina.

His smile made her forget her yogurt parfait. "Omelet?" She dropped her spoon on the table and sprang up. Both Jakob and Annelise looked from her to Marc and back to her. Big knowing smiles started.

"No rush," Marc said.

But there was a hurry and she scurried to the stove. She had no defenses to hold her back from kissing him good morning. Or from throwing her arms around him as Annelise had done to Jakob. Or from simply losing herself in his smile.

"Let me help you," Marc said, moving toward her.

"No, no, sit down. I don't like non-cooks at the stove with me."

"How do you know I'm a non-cook?" He stopped at the counter separating them.

Katrina looked over her shoulder. "Watching Food Network doesn't make you a cook. Sit." She cracked two eggs into a bowl and was glad he moved away. She breathed easier. That was too close for comfort. *He* was too close for comfort. She'd probably forget how to make an omelet with him next to her.

"The snow is brilliant." Marc blinked hard and turned away from the window.

"There's lots of it," Annelise said.

"There most certainly is." He sat at a chair with his back to the window.

"You don't look any worse for the wear," Jakob said. "You showered?"

"I did. The water was a little cool, but I managed."

"What happened to the buttons on your shirt?" Jakob asked.

Marc was quiet. Katrina kept her attention on

whisking the eggs.

"Katrina ripped them off."

Jakob and Annelise laughed. Katrina turned to find Marc smirking and went back to whisking. She couldn't let them see her smile.

"Right," Annelise said, disbelief in her tone.

Good. If Annelise didn't believe it, then neither would Ingrid nor Rebeka.

"I gather the power is back on in this part of the inn," Marc said.

"It is." She poured the eggs into the pan. "Your room won't have any heat until the furnace kicks in there."

"No problem. This looks like a feast."

"It's all amazing," Jakob said. "I could eat the bread all by myself."

"You did," Annelise said.

"There's lots more." Katrina brought them another basket filled with the egg bread.

Marc poured coffee in his cup. "Then I'd better have some before there isn't any more." He reached for the cream but knocked it over. "I'm sorry." He wiped it.

"Not a problem." Katrina took his napkin and cleaned it. "There's more cream, too." She went to the fridge and filled the creamer.

"You okay?" Jakob asked.

"I'm fine." But Marc's voice was so tight it made Katrina wonder if he really was okay. She put the creamer beside him, sneaked a peek, and went back to the stove. He looked pale. He wasn't well.

"You sure?" Jakob asked. "You did hit your head against the air bag. You may have aggravated your concussion."

"We *all* hit our heads against the air bags yesterday, Jakob. Should we all go through concussion protocol?"

Katrina grabbed the butter from the counter. Marc concentrated on stirring the cream in his coffee but a little too vigorously.

Jakob observed him, concern etched in his eyes. "What a night." He kept his tone light. "Great food, great company, and we didn't even feel the lack of heat."

"You got over the overdose?" Annelise asked Marc.

"Your sister tried to kill me but ended up saving me." His tone was light-hearted again. "We need to practice on dancing, Katrina."

Katrina burst into laughter as she peeked at him. She was sure he didn't mean the dancing in bed. That was great.

"In front of the fireplace." Marc didn't hide a brilliant smile. He remembered, too.

"Dancing?" Annelise said. "You danced, Katrina?"

Katrina threw the egg shells in the compost bin. "No hockey indoors." What else could she say?

"Great bread," Marc said. "When did you make all this? I didn't hear you leave."

They needed to change the subject from dancing and was thankful he did. "You were sleeping soundly." She cleared her throat. "It doesn't take me long."

"Where did you sleep, Katrina?" Annelise's lips turned up at the corners, her tone catty.

What a nosy bugger, Katrina thought. "The wing chair."

"The bed," Marc said over her.

Jakob's and Annelise's eyebrows rose.

"I slept first in the wing chair and then in the bed," Katrina said. "It was cold," she added to support her explanation.

"Okey dokey." Both Annelise's and Jakob's smirks grew wider.

"Did you call the coach?" Jakob asked.

"I called last night and told him the situation. I'll try again later." He cut a piece of sausage. "Homemade?" he asked Katrina.

"Of course."

"Anyone go out yet?"

Katrina's cell rang. "Mom?"

"You all okay?"

"Yes, the power came back. Are you still at the hospital?"

"Yes. I slept in an armchair."

"How's Dad?"

"The doctors removed the water from his lungs but he's weak. Once the roads are cleared, I'll come back. Your father will probably spend another night here. The doctors want to keep him under observation."

"But he's going to be okay? He's going to come home?"

"Of course, he will. You know your father. Stubborn even when he's sick. He'll be home in a day or so."

Katrina didn't like the tone of her mother's voice. But then her mother wouldn't lie to her. She would tell her if something was wrong. She was just afraid of her father not getting better. His health always made her uneasy.

"Wait until I give you the go ahead," she told her

mother. "We have to dig ourselves out first and I'm sure the main roads around here won't be done until much later today. We'll call when everything is clear."

"All right. Give my love to the girls."

"You give our love to Dad."

"Will do."

Katrina closed the phone. Everyone was looking at her. "Dad's doing well," she told Annelise. "He's staying another night for observation. Mom is waiting until the roads are cleared to come home." She remembered Marc's omelet. She slid it onto a plate and set it in front of him. She didn't finish her own breakfast, but she didn't want any more. She was afraid for her father.

She glanced surreptitiously at Marc. She was afraid for him, too. He didn't look himself. There wasn't the self-deprecating arrogance or the inflated ego. No twinkle to his eyes and apart from the dancing reference, there was no more light-heartedness to his tone. Did he suffer another concussion as Jakob believed? She didn't know all the symptoms, but she remembered Ingrid had difficulty with lights and concentrating.

But what could she say to him? Go to your room, turn the lights off, and stay there until a doctor clears you? He wasn't a man to be trifled with. What he wanted to do, he did. And what he wanted he got, like her property.

She removed her apron. "I have to dig us out. Are we still on for the tour?"

Marc took her arm. She melted at the warmth and would have slid onto his lap if they were alone. "We are, but you won't dig us out. You have four able-bodied men here to help you. You must have snow plows or snow blowers."

Katrina was taken aback. "We have a blade. It can be hooked up to a pickup truck or snow blower. We also have lots of shovels. But you're guests. I can't ask you to help out."

"You aren't asking us. I'm offering on everyone's behalf. I don't think anyone will object." He eyed Jakob.

"As long as you make some wonderful lunch for us, Katrina," Jakob said. "I'd be happy to clear the snow. Eric and Tyler will feel just like I do."

"I'll help out, too," Annelise said.

"I'll also be out shortly," Marc said.

Jakob leaned toward him. "Oh no you won't. We all hit our heads on the air bags but none of us is recovering from a concussion. I may be the rookie and you may be the veteran, but you're the one who's always telling me to stand up to everyone. I'm now standing up to you." He gulped. "You're staying inside." His voice was a squeak.

Marc's eyes rounded. "Well, well, well. I don't know whether to be proud of you or to scold you."

"I'm just leaning on the side of caution."

"Thank you for your concern, but I'm fine. No light-headedness, no dizziness, only a slight headache, probably due to those Tylenols. But thanks to those same Tylenols, I slept very soundly. You have to stop worrying about a concussion." He cut into his sausage but with too much force.

"I will stop worrying about a concussion when the team doctor clears you. When he does then you can shovel all the snow you want. Until then," Jakob glanced at Katrina. "Until then, I'm sure Katrina can put you to work chopping onions or doing something in here."

Marc held his fork in mid-air. "I don't chop onions. I shovel snow."

Katrina put her hands on her hips. "You have something against onions?"

Marc put his fork and knife down. "I shovel snow."

"Is there anything between chopping onions and shoveling snow?" Jakob asked Katrina.

Katrina thought of it. "Actually, there is. I have the perfect job for the man who doesn't chop onions but wants to shovel snow. A different kind of shoveling."

Chapter Twelve

Marc stared at the ashes in the fireplace. "You've got to be kidding."

Katrina handed him a bucket, handheld shovel, and brush. "You said no onions. Only shoveling. It'll keep you off your sore foot, too."

"You're taking Jakob's word over mine. My foot is fine, *and* I don't have a concussion. I'm symptom-free. I'll do the dishes."

He had a slight headache and his eyes were sensitive to the sun, but then everyone who walked into the kitchen asked to close the blinds. Otherwise, he was good. He had slept well, probably thanks to the Tylenol and of course Katrina. Making love to her excited him as much as relaxed him. He felt good. He felt secure.

He now wanted more of Katrina. He wanted the lovemaking as much as he wanted to be with her, in the kitchen or wherever she went. He wanted her to rethink what she said the night before. That they were only a moment the god of electricity threw together, and it would end in the morning. He was all ready to prove her wrong, but she stuck to her guns. She didn't want anything to do with him *and* she was putting him to work, cleaning the fireplace in the lobby.

How was he going to make her bend to *his* will if she wouldn't let him be with her?

"The dishwasher handles the dishes."

"Fine. Then I will eat my words and chop onions or peel potatoes or do whatever you do to your bread to make it taste so good. I can be your kitchen help and obey your every command—and desire."

The corners of Katrina's lips twitched in a smile. "I prefer to chop my own onions, peel my own potatoes, and knead my own bread, thank you. And you don't want an executive chef barking orders at you while holding knives in her hands."

"I love a challenge, Katrina."

She knocked on the bucket, her expression unrelenting.

"I know what you're doing. You don't want me with you." He remembered his words of the night before. He stared her down. "Are you afraid of me, Katrina Sherrer? Are you afraid we aren't just a moment?"

Katrina put her hands on her hips and moved up to him, staring him right back. She reminded him of his first coach, nicknamed the General and was thankful she held no knives.

"I told you. I don't like non-cooks near my stove. I don't even tolerate anyone in the kitchen who doesn't have to be there. Ask my sisters." She picked up a plastic apron from the coffee table and held it out for him. "You might want to put this on or your nice Armani suit will have soot all over it."

"How do you know it's Armani?"

"I wore it, remember?"

Marc swiped the apron from her. His hope to have Katrina all to himself was not coming true. "This is the kind of job the captain of a team delegates to the juniors."

She poked him in the chest. "I'm the captain of this team, Marc."

His eyebrows shot up and he was sure his eyes twinkled. He moved in closer. "Boss me around somewhere else." *Like in bed* he wanted to say and hoped she understood. "I can be very submissive somewhere else."

She pushed him away. "The vacuum is behind the bar."

Did she just ignore him? "The vacuum?"

"Takes care of any ashes the brush and shovel don't." She strode toward the front desk.

"I'll have you know I'm not happy."

She shrugged, completely indifferent. "It's been noted."

"I'm going to sing."

"You can dance for all I care," she shouted back from somewhere in the kitchen.

"Not without you, Katrina," he shouted back. But there was no retort.

Sighing in resignation, Marc tied the apron around himself and sat at the fireplace. He didn't want to sing or dance. He just wanted to be with Katrina. It was all he wanted since finding her missing from his bed in the morning. He had quickly showered, tolerating the cold water, and dressed, hoping to find her alone, but Jakob and Annelise beat him. Then it went downhill from there with ludicrous talk of concussion symptoms and now shoveling soot and ashes of all things.

Well, he'd corner her. Sooner or later. He'd remind her of their night together and sway her to his way of thinking. If it didn't work, then they had a firm date set for after lunch at precisely three o'clock. Just the two of them. They would drive around the property and she would tell him everything that could make the inn prosperous again.

I'm all over the place, she said to him the night before. He knew. He saw it in everything she did and didn't. There wasn't any need for her to tell him. It was why he suggested the tour of the grounds. It was the only way of giving her hope and showing her how much she meant to him. He would listen to what she said and then make up his mind if her plan proved to be as lucrative as his.

Unfortunately, he didn't think it had any financial merit. But he would listen just the same. He had to show he cared about her. It would score some valuable points and in the long-run, win her over. He wanted to see her. He wanted her in his life.

He shoveled the ashes into the bucket. Soot flew everywhere, making him sneeze. His parents would never believe what he was doing. His brother would never let him live it down.

"You're not doing a good job," Katrina said as she moved through the lobby and into the hall.

"It's messy and tedious." He never did any of this stuff when he was younger. He grabbed the remote from the coffee table and put the TV on, flipping through the channels. Morning talk shows. All-day news. Sports. His kind of thing.

"Cartoons are on." Katrina strode back through the lobby and into the kitchen, holding a bag of what was probably dirty linen.

"Hah, hah, hah." But he got hooked on a cartoon series his youngest nephew raved about before he settled on a sports channel.

When he finished, including vacuuming the fireplace, he went into the kitchen. Katrina was putting on her parka and boots.

"More black?" he asked.

She slipped on a black hat and gloves. "My undies aren't."

"Something to think about." He held up the bucket and brush, evidence of his labor. "All done."

"Now you can put the ashes in the compost bin in the garage. Get your coat. I'll meet you there."

Marc put everything down, threw off the apron, and hurried off to put on his winter gear. He felt like a kid with permission to run outside and play.

He grabbed the pail and went out into a cold day, the snow crunching under his shoes. But the sun was brilliant and hurt his eyes. It was so blinding, it made him lightheaded.

Dammit, this wasn't good. He was supposed to have recovered from his concussion. He needed his sunglasses, but they were in his smashed-up Range Rover and probably in the same condition as his car.

He lowered the toque over his eyes and hurried toward the garage. Katrina was showing Eric how to put the blade on a pickup truck. He emptied the contents of the bucket in the compost bin and moved to the pickup to listen. Once the blade was attached, Eric sat in the driver's seat. Katrina sat beside him and gave him a few lessons on operating the blade.

"Sounds easy enough," Eric said.

Marc opened the door. "Slide over."

Eric stared down at him. "You're on desk duty. Go back to cleaning fireplaces."

"It's done and I'm fine. How hard can it be to drive

and operate the blade?"

"It takes concentration and you've been squinting ever since you came outside. It'll be worse when the sun and the snow ricochet off each other. Now back to the bench. You're sitting this period out."

Marc banged the door shut and moved away, trying not to scowl like a punished boy. Eric lowered the blade and pushed snow from the drive onto the sides.

But he wasn't giving up. He spied the snow blower in the corner and moved to it. Tyler came out of nowhere and delivered one of his infamous body checks. "Have you finished the dishes, bro?"

"It was the fireplace, and it's all clean."

"Then go fold the laundry." Tyler took the snow blower and began moving snow from the less accumulated areas.

Several shovels lay in the corner. He moved toward them but didn't hear Jakob approaching.

"Here you go." Jakob handed him sunglasses. "If you're going to stay out here, at least wear these." He snatched the shovels and moved past him. "Better yet, go back inside and set the table for lunch. I should be getting hungry soon." He gave a shovel to Annelise, Rebeka, and Ingrid and they shoveled the walkways and paths.

Fine. He'd look for Katrina and follow her around like a lost puppy.

He put the sunglasses on. They cut down on the glare and, hopefully would avert any major headache. He had every intention of staying outside and going out with Katrina in the afternoon.

He trudged to the front of the inn, the snow climbing up to his knees and clinging to the bottom of his pants. Katrina came out of the garage, took him by the arm, and led him to the kitchen.

Marc tucked her arm securely under his. "You want me, don't you?" He was sure his smile beamed more brilliantly than the snow.

Katrina smiled sweetly. "I most certainly do." In the kitchen, she removed his coat, sunglasses, and toque. It was a good sign. He snatched a kiss, but she dived away. She removed her parka. "Follow me." She even used her finger to beckon him.

No need to beckon. "With pleasure." He followed her to his room. Now this was the best sign ever. "You want me, I knew it." Her wish was his command.

"I most certainly do." She opened the door and indicated the fireplace. Beside it was a shovel, bucket, brush, and apron.

Marc's smile faded. "You don't play fair."

She blew him a kiss from down the hall. "Neither do you."

She had a point.

He cleaned the fireplace and would have grumbled and complained but there was no one to hear him. He turned the TV on and watched the news. Once finished, he went back into the kitchen, but Katrina was nowhere in sight. Something hit the window. Annelise threw a snowball but it missed Jakob. She threw another and it hit him in the nose. Jakob cleaned his face, but another snowball hit him, followed by a volley.

Enough! He wasn't any fairytale princess ordered to scrub the floors by her evil stepmother. He threw on his coat, toque, gloves, and sunglasses, emptied the ashes in the compost and strode to the front of the inn in search of Katrina. The abandoned pickup truck sat halfway down the drive and the snow blower at the end of the walkway. Eric and Tyler ran past him and joined Jakob and Annelise in slinging snowballs at each other. They threw some at Rebeka and Ingrid. Screaming, they dropped their shovels and a snowball fight ensued.

So far, so good. The sunglasses helped. No onslaught of a headache. Only a minor one. The sun was warming him up instead of picking a fight.

Grabbing an abandoned shovel, Marc hammered at ice around the front doors to the inn. He removed most when Jakob spied him and raced toward him.

"You need to be inside, Marc."

Marc picked up snow with the shovel and threw it at him. But Katrina came around the veranda and the snow landed on her.

Marc gasped as did Jakob.

Katrina stood stock still.

"You look so much better in white," Marc said.

She whipped the snow from her face and coat.

Jakob ran off in a hurry. Marc wanted to do the same but stood his ground. He was not afraid of her.

Not one bit. Really.

"I'm not cleaning out anymore fireplaces. I'm fine and I'm staying outside and in the sun." He hammered at the ice and thought Katrina would protest. He hoped she would tell him to go inside and peel the sweet potatoes on the kitchen counter, but he heard nothing. Was she getting ready to throw snow at him?

He grinned to himself. He'd love to have a snowball fight with her. At least he could grab her. But still he neither heard nor felt anything. He glanced over his shoulder. She was gone.

Shit. His day wasn't going as he wanted at all. His

head throbbed, and he was nowhere near getting close to Katrina.

Chapter Thirteen

As agreed, after lunch, Marc bundled himself up and found Katrina putting on her winter wear in the kitchen. The guys had removed a lot of the snow from around the inn and now played hockey with Katrina's sisters on a makeshift rink. They didn't have any skates or hockey sticks and slid around on their boots or shoes, using branches and rocks to play.

He moved toward the window. "Looks like the snow crew is on an extended break. Shouldn't we wait until they've cleared a little more snow?"

She slipped on high boots. Black, of course. "We don't need any snow cleared the way we're going."

"You have a snowmobile?"

"Something better."

He put on his gloves and sunglasses and followed her outside, past the makeshift ice rink where Annelise just scored on Tyler and toward the back of the inn. He had spied some roofs but never noticed the barns and a small corral.

Katrina unlocked the doors of the first barn. Marc was surprised to see a stable with a number of stalls. He moved inside and laughed, stopping at the middle stalls where four horses chewed hay and drank water.

"I never even saw these barns—or stable." He stroked the nozzle of the first horse with a white mane. "They're all beauties. They don't look any worse for the wear after last night. It's pretty warm in here."

"The barn is well insulated, and it has its own heater and generator. We could have slept comfortably in here if we had to."

"You didn't sleep comfortably?"

Katrina smirked as she opened the door of the stall holding the horse with the white mane. She rubbed the horse on the neck. The horse drew its face closer. "You want a kiss? You got it." Katrina kissed it between the eyes

"I've wanted a kiss all morning and I got nothing," Marc said.

"It was morning. All back to the way it was as I said last night."

"Yes, but a kiss and a little bit more was supposed to change everything."

Katrina shook her head and moved to the other stalls. "I see you all managed well," she said to the horses, stroking them one by one on the neck through the gates. "Girls, meet Marc." The horses neighed or kicked at straw. "Yes, he's a looker—I admit it—but he's not your type. He only has two legs."

Marc ambled down the stable, but all the other stalls were empty. "Who takes care of them?"

"My father for the most part. We had ten horses but sold them except for these four. They belong to my sisters and me, and my dad is letting us decide what to do with them. So far, we haven't been able to part with them. This one with the brown patch on her forehead is Principessa. The first one with the white mane is Mistress Snow. This dark one is Rosiebelli, and this last one who fidgets far too much is Macaroon. My sisters and I named them."

"Let me guess. Yours is Macaroon?"

"Good guess."

He took her in his arms to give her the long kiss denied him all day, but she slipped away. "Ah, come on. Not even for old times' sake?"

"Not in front of the ladies."

"So, if we were alone—"

"Nope." She turned to the horses. "Ladies, are you ready for a little exercise?"

They responded with stamping or shuffling.

"I haven't ridden a horse in a number of years," Marc said. "I don't think I could manage one in snow."

Katrina took Rosiebelli out of her stall. "Who said anything about riding a horse?" She led the horse out of the stable and toward another barn. She held a key out for Marc who unlocked the door and swung it open.

Marc's eyebrows rose as he stared at a beautiful red-wood sleigh, which could sit at least eight people. "This is a gorgeous piece of work." He caressed the swirls carved into the body. "Your father made it?"

"My great grandfather. But my grandfather and father maintained it."

The barn appeared to be a wood-working studio with saws of various sizes, drills, routers, lumber, and so much more Marc couldn't name. "Is this your father's workshop?"

Katrina hooked Rosiebelli to the sleigh. "It is. Or should I say, it was. My dad also used it to train apprentices and youth from around the area."

"He was involved with community work?" Marc felt ashamed. He only did what the front office staff asked. "It looks pretty clean. I don't even see sawdust. I assume he hasn't been here since his heart attack."

"Longer. Over a year. He misses the youth. They never wanted to get their hands dirty and then found they loved creating with wood. A lot were at-risk youth. Sometimes the carpentry turned their lives around. They went to college or took on other apprentice jobs."

She finished harnessing Rosiebelli.

"Can I help?"

"Mistress Snow and Principessa go next."

They took the two horses and while she gave him instructions, he hooked each horse up to the harness. Satisfied he was doing it well, she went back for Macaroon, who he harnessed without any direction from her.

"Do we need all four horses pulling us and the sleigh?" he asked.

"No, but they haven't exercised for a while and this will do them good." She climbed onto the bench and took the reins. "Can you close the doors after me?" She pulled on the reins and the horses moved out of the barn.

Marc closed the doors and climbed next to Katrina. "What's in the last barn?" He indicated the barn with gleaming wooden paneling and red double doors. "It looks too clean to hold animals or to be another carpenter's workshop."

"It's a kitchen."

"You cook in there?"

She didn't answer for a long time as though evading the question. "We set it up to parallel what my father was doing with carpentry and the youth. To teach cooking to at-risk youths."

"I assume you were the teacher and the instigator."

She made a brief nod. "I was going to be one of the

teachers. There were several others from King Court and the reserve who wanted to help out. But it's incomplete. We originally used the kitchen in the inn and I found I loved teaching the kids. As expected, they would come in with attitude but after a couple classes, they gave in and enjoyed cooking. Several youths went on to culinary school."

"You are an angel."

"Far from it. When things fell apart at the inn and restaurant, we put the Kitchen-in-the-Barn program, the name it was supposed to be called, on hold."

"It's unfortunate. Both programs sound wonderful."

"*Sounded* wonderful. Past tense. Can't bring the programs with us. Wherever that'll be." Katrina steered the horses past the barns. "Everything in the barns will be sold along with what we have in the inn and restaurant."

Sadness crept into her voice again. Time to change the subject. He wanted this to be a constructive drive not a gloomy one. "Are you going to show me how to drive or whatever the term is to steer these ladies and the sleigh?"

"If you'd like to, and drive is good enough. But I'll do the honors first. It takes a little maneuvering around the corral and out of the inn." The horses pulled them past the makeshift rink. The instant the guys saw them, they dropped their pretend hockey sticks and raced over with Katrina's sisters.

"Are you two on some private outing?" Eric asked.

"Are we?" Marc hoped Katrina would say yes.

"Grab the blankets from the stable and hop on," Katrina said, deflating Marc's hope.

Her sisters rushed back to the stable and returned with several blankets. They got into the sleigh and covered themselves.

"Tally ho," Tyler said.

"That's only used for fox hunts, bro," Jakob replied. "Onward, Dasher, Prancer, Vixen and everyone else." Katrina took them past the corral and into a vast land of field, hill, and forest covered in thick undisturbed snow, glistening ice, and pockets of evergreen trees. The landscape looked like an idyllic postcard of a winter wonderland.

"This is beautiful land," Marc said.

"It most certainly is. And it has so much potential." They got to several huge mounds, which looked like baby hills with valleys, flat patches of land, and several frozen brooks. "A golf course would be ideal here," Katrina said. "It's flat with just enough little hills and ponds." They continued until they got to several hills of various heights. "Skiing wouldn't be too practical, but snow tubing and snowboarding would work very well here. The hills aren't big or dangerous but enough for a family to enjoy themselves. Several cabins or chalets could be put in just there on the flat piece of land for private vacations. Cross-country skiing would be wonderful."

They continued for another stretch, while her sisters and the guys sang snow songs. They arrived at a lake, simmering with ice. "We don't have any fish here. The lake was hand made before I was born. A water park with slides would work well here. It's shallow in some ends and deeper in others. Just farther off the lake narrows. Canoes could be put in for leisurely paddles, too."

She directed the sleigh to an area with trees. Some were evergreen, but the majority were massive oak and maple trees. They were bare but coated with thick ice and shimmered like gems. "We had a trail here once. People used it to walk or cycle or jog, but it's overgrown now. It could be reconstructed and a trail for horseback riding added. The stable at the inn can be made larger to house more than ten horses. We have room enough to also add a stall for those guests who want to bring their own horses. And, of course, we could have horse sleighs in the winter along with ski-dooing and snowshoeing, and hay rides in the summer. We can do so much more than the other two resorts in the area can. Our property is vast with so much more personality and charisma."

Marc remained quiet. He envisioned everything Katrina did. But no matter what she said, all he saw were the incredible number of houses and roads he could build. He could even envision the families with kids, playing street hockey.

Her vision had merit and offered long-term monetary gain, but his plan of a housing development, exploded with immediate financial gain. Far more than any lodge could ever make for him or the other investors.

But how could he tell her?

He was glad his eyes were hidden behind the sunglasses.

He set out to give Katrina hope but would only pull it away from her. He set out to win her over, but he lost her even before he had her. He didn't know what to do or what was worse. Giving her hope or taking it all back. He was a fraud.

Katrina didn't say much as she steered the sleigh back to the barn. She offered the reins to him, but he declined. He said he preferred to lay back, enjoy the ride, and leave the work to her. He lost interest in driving and his head throbbed. How could he take the reins and let her teach him when he was going to rob her of everything precious to her? He could suggest a financial evaluation and have an accounting firm do a quick one. She had a few more weeks before she had to declare bankruptcy. In the meantime, he could see her with the hope of winning her over and lessening the pain when she eventually signed those papers.

Once they got back to the barn, Eric jumped off the sleigh to open the doors. "Marc, we're going to make such a fortune. Can you imagine all the houses we can build on this land? How much money we're going to make? The place is even bigger than I thought. You were right. We're going to make mega millions. Oh, I'm sorry, Katrina."

Katrina shook his remarks off. Her face was red from the cold and wind but there was no emotion in her eyes.

Marc hated what he was about to say, but it had to be said. He couldn't be a fraud. He owed her the truth. "Yes, I can imagine."

Chapter Fourteen

Katrina jumped off the bench.

Marc was at her side. "But as promised I will give you a financial evaluation. It will be a simple one. You're running out of time."

Katrina said nothing as she unharnessed Macaroon.

"Off hand, your plan offers long-term financial gain but short-term losses." He waited but she said nothing. "Many short-term financial losses. That's the problem."

She led the horse to the stable and he followed.

Marc stood by the doors and watched Katrina move Macaroon into the stall. "The evaluation will say exactly what I am saying." The horse raised its nose to Katrina, but she didn't acknowledge it. "I'll have the evaluation for you by the end of the week."

"I'll look forward to it."

Marc sighed but he was far from relieved. If she wasn't open to him now when he promised her what she wanted, how would she feel once he gave her the actual evaluation? It would only confirm what he said but in hard cold numbers. If she didn't look at him now, would she look at him then?

She wouldn't want anything to do with him.

Annelise came up beside him. "We'll bring in the other girls and the sleigh, too, Katrina. We'll clean them up."

Katrina closed the gate on Macaroon. "Thank you. I'm making dinner." She moved past them and stomped through the snow to the kitchen door.

Marc rubbed his forehead. He needed his medication before his headache worsened. "Does Katrina always run off to the kitchen when she's upset?"

"Katrina always runs off to the kitchen when she wants to be alone," Annelise said, taking Jakob's hand as he stopped at her side. "It's her sanctuary. What happened between the two of you?"

He updated her and Jakob.

"The inn is a dying cause," Annelise said. "She says she's holding on because she thinks my father will die if she sells. Frankly, I think he's waiting for her to sell so he can get better and move on. I'm sure she's holding on because it's her mess and she wants to see if she can salvage it."

Marc was surprised as much as alarmed. "What do you mean her mess?"

"She was the one who suggested the renovations in the first place—not to the extent my parents went to, but she did want to renovate and modernize everything. She wanted it to become competitive while still holding on to its original look and feel and its five-star rating. Her restaurant would have complemented the five-stars. With her culinary skills and drive, she would earn the restaurant a three-star in no time. It would all be idyllic."

"So she thinks it's her fault the inn died and now you have to sell?"

"Yup."

"Frankly, it was a smart idea. She was smart."

"But the idea backfired on her."

"Not everything in business is a sure thing. Her vision wasn't your parents'." Marc admired her for trying. Some people never took risks and lived to regret it. He was proud of her. She was like him. A challenger. A risk-taker. She didn't sit around and do nothing. "She could make it at any other restaurant."

"You tell her."

He had. She didn't want to start at the bottom again and he understood. In actuality, she lost all her confidence. In her culinary skills and in herself. She lost her ego. It took a beating and was badly bruised. He saw the whole picture now. If she signed, she would admit failure.

If only she knew how proud he was of her. He didn't see her as a failure but as a go-getter. She would survive and do very well. He was more certain of her success than ever before.

He saw her through the window, moving around in the kitchen, getting things out of the fridge. A big man appeared, overshadowing the doorway, leading from the family's apartment to the kitchen. "There's a man in there!" He raced to Katrina but Annelise held him back.

"It's Lowan. He's a good friend of the family."

"He has access to the inn?"

"Whenever he's around he helps my dad and Katrina with the ground maintenance."

Marc watched as Lowan removed his toque and parka. The man was huge. Probably taller than him and built like one of those world wrestler-entertainers he watched as a child. "He's a monster."

"Lowan?" Annelise laughed. "You haven't seen him up close. He's gorgeous and a real nice guy. He's

Mr. September for the King Court Calendar of Men."

Marc hadn't glanced at the other men in the calendar. He'd take a look if Mr. September was his competition and it appeared, he was. The kitchen was off-limits to everyone except those who needed to be there, but the ninth-month calendar guy was there. "Why is he allowed to enter Katrina's sanctuary?"

"They're good friends. Katrina and his sister Olivia, who also happens to be the inn's lawyer, went to school together and are besties. His grandmother was a cook at the inn. She and Katrina were really close."

"Are you talking about the woman from the reserve? The woman who was Katrina's inspiration?"

"Yes, that's right. Lowan's grandmother. Lowan does a lot of work on the reserve when he isn't filming, and he's a pretty good cook himself."

"Filming?" Was the man an actor?

"Is that Lowan Beach?" Jakob moved closer. "The half-man, half-android captain on *Intergalactic Wars*?"

"The one and only."

"He's Canadian?"

"He is. When he isn't filming, he spends time with his family in King Court. His dad and mine set up the carpentry training program for the at-risk youth many years ago. My dad used to hire exclusively from the reserve to work in the inn or on the grounds and it worked in everyone's favor. Lowan is a mentor for some of those youth."

Marc's competition was not only some charismatic actor but a saint. How was he supposed to hate a saint? He did charity work for the hockey team but only what was asked and nothing more. He was at a disadvantage. He felt small. It was a first for him. He could do so much more. Mr. September did.

"There aren't any more training programs here at the inn. Why is he still coming around?" He was sure he had motives, extending beyond friendship with Katrina.

Shit, he needed his medication. His headache was worse. He couldn't even think straight—or was it because of Katrina and the monster-actor-saint in her kitchen?

"His younger sister Megan fell in with the wrong crowd. Lowan and Olivia pulled her out and Katrina put her to work in the kitchen. She washed the dishes and cooked some basic recipes. She loved cooking so much she helped Katrina with the youth and is in culinary school now. Soon after, Katrina opened the kitchen to other youths and renovated the barn for the program. Lowan probably came to see if he could help plow the snow."

"It's done." Marc glanced at the drive. It looked like a multi-humped hill of snow. "Mostly. By amateurs. He can go home."

"They're good friends, Marc," Annelise said with a big knowing smile.

"He's too friendly to be a good friend."

"How about brother then? We all grew up together."

Lowan put his arms around Katrina. Marc's hands tightened into fists. "Is that really necessary?" Katrina looked up at him, telling him what she wasn't telling Marc. Lowan nodded. Commiserating.

"Take him out, Jakob."

Jakob laughed. "I'd rather go get his autograph—and a selfie."

Lowan walked to the window and waved at Annelise. She and Jakob waved back as Marc curtly nodded. Lowan indicated he was coming out.

"He's a big Montreal fan," Annelise said as though to appease him. "He, his dad and mine often watched the big games together."

It was hard not to like the guy.

"I'm getting his autograph," Jakob said. "Eric, Tyler, Captain Borgman is here."

Eric and Tyler were bringing the horses to the stables. "Captain Borgman from *Intergalactic Wars*?" Eric asked.

"One and only."

Eric made some crazy salute and said something sounding gibberish but was probably the make-believe language associated with the series.

Rebeka and Ingrid explained Lowan to Eric and Tyler. Both became excited as boys about to meet their hockey idol.

Tyler pulled Mistress Snow into the stable. "Be right there."

Annelise took Marc's arm. "Did Katrina break my dad's cardinal rule last night? No sex under the roof of the inn?"

Marc didn't acknowledge. He was trying to telepathically get Katrina to drop Lowan's hands and kick him out of the kitchen.

"She did," Annelise laughed. "Now I understand what kind of dancing you did."

Jakob pulled the sunglasses off Marc. "And I was afraid you aggravated your concussion again." He punched him in the arm. "You danced."

Marc pushed the sunglasses back on. "I'm fine."

But his vision was blurry, and it upset him.

"You worked some magic on her."

"The magic was a one-time deal." Marc adjusted the toque over his forehead. "I want it to be more, but she runs off the minute she sees me coming. She won't let me be in the only place I know for sure she'll be. The kitchen." He watched Katrina and Lowan. Lowan went into the pantry and brought her back a basket of vegetables. "He's brought her carrots, potatoes, and onions." Lowan picked up something on the counter and a carrot from the basket. "He's peeling carrots for her." He should be the one—the only one—peeling carrots for her. He'd even endure onions.

Jakob and Annelise laughed.

"It's horrible," Jakob managed to say. "You're even going to eat the carrots he's peeling."

Katrina took the peeler away from Lowan. He refused to hand over the carrot but finally did and put on his parka and hat. He kissed her on the cheek and went to the kitchen door. He stepped out to meet them.

Marc's blood boiled. He didn't want to meet him. He didn't watch the sci-fi series his hockey buddies did. And now he had to play nice with Mr. September.

Ingrid and Rebeka rushed to greet him, followed closely by Eric and Tyler, who each shook Lowan's hand eagerly.

Marc turned back to Katrina. She took the carrots from the basket and peeled them with as much concentration as writing an exam.

"You want the magic to continue?" Annelise asked. "You want to get near her?"

"Is it possible?" Marc asked. "I don't have access to her sanctuary like Mr. Borgman."

"*Captain* Borgman," Jakob said, rushing off to meet him.

Annelise took his arm and lead him to Mr. September. "I have an idea, Mr. Dancing-Man January."

Chapter Fifteen

Marc stood by the front desk and put his earbuds in his ears. "Can you hear me?"

"I can hear you," Annelise said, from Jakob's room.

"Hear you loud and clear, *mon capitaine*," Jakob whispered, also from his room. "Or would you prefer Big Eagle?"

Marc ignored him.

"You ready?" Annelise asked.

He had taken his medication. He was headache-free and eager to get things going. "I'm ready." With his cell in his hand, looking like he was listening to music, he walked into the huge industrial-sized kitchen. Katrina chopped carrots with a massive knife. Her eyes told him he was invading her territory. He gulped. He was but for a good cause. His.

"You can't be hungry," she said.

"No, I'm good. For now."

She didn't resume chopping the carrots. "You know I don't like people in my kitchen who can't cook or help me while I'm cooking."

"Who says I can't cook?" Apart from scrambled eggs, toasted bread, pasta, and the occasional barbecued steak, he couldn't cook. His housekeeper prepared his meals.

"Well thank you, but I have everything under

control. I don't need your help."

"I thought I could make some tea."

Her eyebrows rose in question. She looked like she didn't believe he drank tea. He normally didn't but if it would get him close to Katrina, he'd do whatever was necessary.

"The kettle is on the counter." She indicated it with her big knife. "We have an assortment of teas in the cabinet on the left."

"How about scones?"

She was about to chop and stopped. "You want scones?" She took a deep breath but settled herself. She probably remembered she was the hostess who couldn't be nasty to the irritating guest. Him. "I'll make a batch right after the vegetables are cut."

"No need. I can make them. Then maybe we can have them with some tea. Together."

He threw in the "together" at the last minute. She didn't scream "no". It was a good sign. He aroused her interest or disbelief. Whatever the case, he now had to go through with the plan.

"You know how to make scones?"

"Of course. Do you like them?"

She put the knife down and scooped the carrots into a big pan. "Plain."

"Best kind."

She took the skins off onions.

Marc cleared his throat. It was the sign, signaling Annelise and Jakob. He was ready.

"Get an apron from the kitchen door," Annelise told him.

He looked around, pretending ignorance. One peeked from behind the door. He rolled up his jacket sleeves, put on the apron, washed his hands, and waited for further instructions.

"Get the flour from the pantry," Annelise said. "It's the room with the white double doors. The other doors, the swinging ones, lead to the restaurant."

"I assume the flour is in there?" Marc asked Katrina, indicating the pantry.

"It is."

He went to the pantry. It was massive, bigger than his room in the inn. A lot of the shelves were empty or close to bare but there was a shelf of flour—at least ten types of flour. All-purpose, cake and pastry, bread, self-rising, corn, coconut, almond, rye, sorghum of all things—crap, who knew there were so many kinds of flour. "You have many types of flour here," he called out to Katrina, but it was Annelise who needed to hear him.

"I'm a chef."

"Get the all-purpose flour," Annelise said.

He found it and brought it to the counter on the opposite end from where Katrina chopped onions. "May I use this space?"

"It's all yours."

"Grab a large bowl," Annelise said. "They should be under the counter you're working at."

He peered below the counter and found one large yellow bowl.

"Add three hundred and fifty grams of flour in the bowl," Jakob said. "*Mon* Big Eagle *capitaine*," he added with a laugh.

Three hundred and fifty grams? How the heck would he know three hundred and fifty grams?

"Use the kitchen scale to measure it," Annelise

said. "Katrina has several on a shelf near the fridge."

He spied one and took it to his space on the counter. He pressed a couple buttons until the screen read grams. He put the bowl on it, but it jumped to four hundred and seventy-five grams. He wasn't sure what to do.

Katrina eyed him as she added the onions to the pan with the carrots.

He pressed the button with "weight" written under it until the screen returned to zero grams. Relieved he added flour until it measured three hundred and fifty grams.

"Now add one quarter teaspoon of salt and one teaspoon of baking powder. The baking powder should be in the pantry somewhere close to the flour. Measuring spoons are in a drawer next to the stove. Use a fork to mix it all together." Marc found the measuring spoons and a fork, grabbed the salt and baking powder from the pantry, and mixed them into the flour.

"Okay, now get the butter from the fridge," Jakob said. "You're going to need eighty-five grams. The recipe says to cut them into small squares then put them in the flour and using your fingers, rub them into the flour until the mixture looks like fine crumbs."

He grabbed the butter, measured eighty-five grams on the scale, cut it into small squares as directed, and threw them into the flour. He didn't like the idea of mixing with his hands, but he had to show he'd done this many times before. He plunged his hands into the flour mixture and crumbled the butter.

Katrina observed him on and off as she sautéed the onions with carrots. "Where did you learn to make scones?"

"My Great Aunt Hazel. She married my grandfather's brother. Born and raised in Sussex, England, before she fell in love with Great Uncle Samuel. I stayed with them when I played in Toronto as a teen and helped her out in the kitchen." The truth of the matter was Great Aunt Hazel was a terrible cook. She always bought scones and they would sit in the living room and eat them with raspberry jam and clotted cream while watching old musicals on TV.

"Is the butter the size of peas yet?" Annelise asked.

"This was my job," Marc said. "Cutting in the butter until they were the size of stones and then peas." He rubbed his hands together to let the flour mixture fall into the bowl. He was surprised his hands weren't slick with butter. There was only a film on his fingers. "Just right."

"Good," Annelise said. "Now add three tablespoons of caster sugar and mix it in with your hands, too."

"Caster sugar?"

Katrina thought he asked her. "I ran out. Regular sugar will work just fine."

"Great Aunt Hazel swore by caster sugar, but I suppose regular sugar will have to do." He added the sugar as instructed.

"Now add one hundred and seventy-five milliliters of milk but it should be warmed a little," Jakob said. "Don't make it hot. The recipe says tepid."

Tepid? Marc remembered old movies where the mother tested the baby's formula on her wrist to make sure it wasn't hot or cold but just right. Tepid.

He measured the milk and popped it into the microware. He took it out after thirty seconds and touched it with his finger. Seemed tepid to him. He tested it on his wrist. Tepid enough.

"You're running low on milk," Marc told Katrina, but to remind Annelise and Jakob for more instructions.

"I'll put it on the grocery list."

"Okay. What else did Aunt Hazel put in?" he said aloud, as though recalling the recipe from all those times they made it together.

"I don't know about Aunt Hazel," Annelise said, "But now you have to add one teaspoon of vanilla extract—I think it's in the fridge, and a squeeze of lemon into the milk mixture. Lemons are in the pantry."

He went to the fridge but couldn't find the vanilla. It was like looking in a walk-in closet for a shoe lace. "Do you have vanilla extract?"

Katrina came up beside him, grabbed it, and handed it to him. She looked down at the mixture but didn't say anything.

"I need a shot of lemon." He found lemons in the pantry, cut one in half, and squeezed the juice into the milk mixture along with the vanilla. Katrina looked at him curiously.

"My aunt swore lemon juice added to the flavor."

Katrina shrugged as she removed a big pot from the stove and dumped the hot liquid into a colander in the sink. Potatoes tumbled out.

"Okay," Annelise said. "Set the oven to four hundred and fifty degrees and put a cookie sheet inside. It's supposed to get warm. Baking sheets are under the counter. Use the top oven."

Marc put the cookie sheet inside the oven and set the temperature. He went back to the bowl and stared down at it, waiting for the next set of instructions.

"Okay." He waited. Where were Annelise and Jakob? What was the next set of instructions? He cleared his throat as though something were stuck. "Did I remember everything?" he said aloud.

"Sorry," Annelise said.

"My bad," Jakob said. "I kind of, well, I actually did give Annelise a kiss."

"Make a well in the center and add the milk mixture," Annelise said. "Then stir it into a ball with a fork.

He stirred the mixture until it came together into a ball.

"Okay, now spread a little flour on the counter, turn the dough onto it, and bring it together until it's smooth. It shouldn't take more than a couple turns. Flatten it out with your hands or a rolling pin to about four centimeters deep."

He did as he was told, using his hands. No rolling pin for a supposed master of scones.

"Now, use a round cookie cutter or the mouth of a glass. Dip the cutter or glass opening in flour and cut out as many rounds as will come out—there should be eight if you did everything right. Take the cookie sheet out of the oven and put them on it. Be careful. It's going to be hot."

Marc used a towel to grab the baking sheet and set it down beside the batter.

"Once done, grab an egg from the fridge, beat it, and brush the tops of the scones with it," Annelise said. "There should be all sorts of pastry brushes in one of the drawers. You're going to have to ask Katrina which brush she uses for the egg wash. She has lots and is very particular about them. You don't want to upset her, do you?"

No, he most certainly did not want to upset her by using the wrong pastry brush. Marc beat the egg. "Do you have a brush to put the egg glaze on the scones?"

Katrina was about to roll out dough but washed her hands, pulled open a drawer, and handed him a brush.

"Thank you."

He brushed the egg glaze on the tops. He stood back and brushed some around the sides. Why not? Once done, he put the bowl and pastry brush down. He was impressed. They looked good.

"Now if the oven has reached four hundred and fifty, put the scones in and let them bake for about ten minutes or until they're golden brown on top. Then you can take them out and if they're good, you and Katrina will have high tea with scones."

"And maybe more, Big Eagle," Jakob said.

That was the idea. Marc put the scones in the oven and washed his hands.

Katrina looked at him. He wasn't sure what she thought.

"Aunt Hazel liked English Breakfast," he said. "I'm an Earl Grey kind of man. But both of us loved the scones with raspberry jam and clotted cream."

Katrina focused on flattening her dough. But he saw a little smile on her face.

As the scones baked, he washed his utensils, cleaned the counter, and even asked if he could wash the pot used for the potatoes. She didn't object, and he scoured it to a shine. He needed all the points he could get.

He dried the pot. "What are you making?"

"Tourtière. My version of it."

"I don't remember the last time I had it." The timer on his phone went off. He left the pot on the counter and checked the scones. They were golden brown. They were done.

He pulled them out, inhaled them, and set them on the counter to cool. He couldn't believe he made them. "Not bad. Not like Great Aunt Hazel's but comparable."

He thought he saw another small smile on Katrina's lips.

Time for tea now. He poured water in the kettle and while it boiled, he grabbed two cups and saucers, two plates, and a teapot from a large buffet. There was an assortment of teas in containers. He pulled out the Earl Grey one but to his dismay found it was loose.

Now what? He didn't know how much to add. "How do you like your tea, Katrina?"

"Not too strong. Earl Grey is fine with me."

"Only one teaspoon per cup," Annelise said.

They were still on the line. Thank goodness.

"Are you going to invite us?" Jakob asked. "I can smell those scones from the lobby."

Marc took out his cell, pretended he was shuffling for a song, cut the connection, and removed his earbuds. That was the answer to Jakob's question.

He added several teaspoons of the tea leaves to the pot followed by the boiling water. "How do you take your tea, Katrina"

"Just milk."

He poured some milk in a little jug and remembered Great Aunt Hazel always warmed the milk. That wasn't imaginary. She swore by it. He set it in the microwave and put the warm milk on the table, too. Katina did her chef business with the dough, but her smile got harder to hide. "Only warm milk for hot tea."

He touched the scones. They were still hot, but he put them on a plate. He found some jam and the clotted cream in the fridge and put them on the table. "Tea is ready."

He didn't think Katrina would stop making the tourtière and join him but to his surprise, she washed her hands and sat down. He poured warm milk in their cups, followed by the tea, and put a scone on her plate and one on his.

Katrina held the scone in her palm and weighed it. She broke it in half and examined it. She was a chef through and through. She took a small bite and chewed it like she was appraising fine wine.

He was on the edge of his chair. Was it good? Did he win her over? This was worse than waiting for the coach to tell him what he did wrong. "Well?"

She waited until she finished chewing. "Your great aunt Hazel taught you well."

Marc wanted to do a fist pump but acknowledged with a nod, which he hoped showed how humble Aunt Hazel's teachings made him.

Katrina put the scone down, moved to the window, and closed the blinds. "Is the kitchen door locked?"

Marc was confused. "No."

She returned to the table. "Lock it. You were a complete turn on."

Chapter Sixteen

Marc sat on the chair, his pants on the floor, his apron covering him up. Katrina got off him, pulled up her panties and pants, and smoothed out her apron.

If he knew baking scones was the secret to disarming a woman and getting her to throw herself at him, he would have tried it long before today.

"Tea's cold," he said.

Katrina smirked. "You're not good for me, Marc."

He stood and pulled on his pants. "You're doing a fine job fooling me. I'll have you know I've never made Great Aunt Hazel's scones for any other woman before."

"I'm flattered, but I'll have you know I've never done it with a man under this roof before or in the kitchen. In any kitchen as a matter of fact. You're making me break too many rules. I hate you even more than before."

Marc laughed in satisfaction. He was on top of the world. If he kept cooking, he might win her over for good. "Would I still be a turn on if you liked me?"

"Yes."

"Would I still be a turn on if I didn't make scones for you?"

She thought for a long time. "It was a great garnish."

He moved toward her, but she rushed to the

counter and her pies. "I have to think about my *tourtières*, Marc."

"*Tourtières* over me?"

She whipped an egg in a bowl, keeping her gaze down, but her lips curled in a smile. He was disarming her.

"You'll have the financial analysis for me by the end of the week?" she asked.

"By the end of the week," he all but sang.

She picked up the dough and arranged it on the baking plate. "Fine. I'll look at it and if it shows my suggestions won't turn a profit until light years away, then I'll sign those papers right after. You'll have won and the land will be yours."

"I'll have won nothing if you don't want to see me after those papers are signed."

Katrina put another pie crust in a second pan. "Let's leave what happens after I sign to—the gods."

It wasn't a yes, but it wasn't a no, either. It's all he could hope for. He was happy but afraid of the financial analysis. It would say what he did. She might go cold again and push him out of her life.

Or maybe she wouldn't if he won her over and softened her. Only time would tell.

His cell startled him. It was the coach. "Greetings, Jacques."

"Greetings to you, too, Marc. How you doing?"

"I'm good."

"Your ankle?"

"It's bruised. Should heal in the next couple of days."

"What about your head?"

"Symptom free." It was an outright lie, but the

team doctor could only confirm the diagnosis.

"And your business buddies, aka your teammates?"

"No complaints from anyone. They shoveled snow and even had a little scrimmage without skates with some lovely-looking opponents. They're keeping active."

"How interesting," he replied with a laugh. "But I need to make sure everyone is all right. Doctor Harrison said you would probably be ready to play next week, and I want to make sure you're still on track."

"I'm ready to play now."

"I'm sure you are but only Doctor Harrison can make the call. I'm sending a helicopter to come and get you all."

"A helicopter?"

Katrina stopped glazing the pies.

"We're all doing well, Jacques. My car is totaled but we planned to get a rental and leave first thing in the morning when the roads are cleared. They didn't plow here yet. You don't need to send a helicopter to retrieve us. We're doing really well." He glanced at Katrina. "Better than well."

"I need to make sure none of you are just saying what I want to hear. We're in for our toughest run after the all-star break and you know as well as I do, we're not too far from first place. With everyone on board and healthy once again we can make it deep into the playoffs."

"One more night won't make a difference. It'll even be beneficial." He lifted the cell from his ear and strode to the window. He thought he heard a helicopter. He opened the blinds. He was right. It was getting closer. This could not be happening. His gaze jumped to Katrina. He needed more time to win her over before she signed those papers. Otherwise, she might crawl back into herself and shut him out. "Please, Jacques. One more night."

"Too late," Jacques said. "I've already sent one. Doctor Harrison will be on board, too."

"Doctor Harrison is on board?" This was worse. He didn't want the doctor to check him. He didn't want to hear what he already knew.

"He'll check you all out there before you fly out. I'll see you all for dinner."

Marc closed the phone.

"You won't be staying for dinner?" Katrina asked.

He shook his head. "I'm sorry. Coach's orders." He strode toward her. "It doesn't change anything between us. I'll bring the evaluation up myself. I'll keep in touch. I want to see you."

Katrina took out the plastic wrap and sealed the *tourtières*. She kept her face averted.

"You don't believe me, do you?"

She gave him a cursory glance. "Is it really going to happen? You might bring up the evaluation in person—if you can get away from your hockey schedule, but us? Really?"

He moved to her side. "Why is it so hard to believe? Or do you think I'm just an opportunistic like your last infamous ex?"

"No, of course not."

"You don't sound convincing to me."

She picked up a tourtière and moved to the fridge, putting distance between them. "You should get ready for the doctor."

"Katrina?"

165

"I'm being realistic, Marc."

"I want you to be truthful."

Katrina picked up the second pie and put it in the fridge, too.

"I will come back—for you. I want to know what we can be together. I think we can be something."

"Enough, Marc." She slammed the fridge door shut. "You're a businessman before you're anything else. Excuse me, you're a hockey player first, a businessman second, and everything else is somewhere down the line. You don't have to pretend with me. You came for one thing and one thing only. The rest was a bonus. We were a moment and nothing else. I have no regrets." She removed her apron and disappeared into the lobby.

Marc watched her leave. Was that how she really saw him? Was that how everyone saw him? That couldn't be him, could it? If it was, it would be a first, but he didn't like himself.

Chapter Seventeen

Tyler and Eric sat glumly in the wing chairs around the fireplace as Jakob leaned against it. They were in Marc's room. Doctor Harrison, a lanky man somewhere close to his seventies, had his hands on his hips and his back to Marc, who sat on the bed. The fireplace blazed, and a portable heater warmed up the room, too. But the room felt cold with Doctor Harrison's disapproval.

He stared Tyler, Eric, and Jakob down. "You three amigos were very lucky to get away with cuts and bruises. Don't know how you did it, especially you, Tyler. You could have easily broken your finger again. I saw the condition of the car and I want to keep the three of you under observation for the next few days. I want to make sure none of you suffered any form of concussion."

Eric sat up straight. "But we don't have any of the symptoms—no nausea, dizziness, sensitivity, sluggishness." He stopped to think of more symptoms. "None of them."

"If none of you display anything in the next few days, then you're all good to go next week, even you, Tyler."

Tyler made a fist punch. "Just what I want to hear."

"Now get out of here. All of you." Doctor Harrison turned to Marc. "You're next."

Jakob, Tyler, and Eric hurried out like penitent

boys, closing the door after them.

Doctor Harrison moved to the edge of the bed. "Do we start with the ankle or the head?"

Marc kicked off his shoes and moved against the pillow. He didn't want to hear anything about the possibility of another concussion. He was already upset about Katrina. He had no idea what to say to make her believe in his sincerity. "The ankle."

Doctor Harrison waited. "You going to take off your sock?"

Marc didn't want to bend. His head would feel like it was falling off. He lifted his knee and pulled his sock to the end of his toes.

Doctor Harrison examined the ankle. "It's a little swollen. Does it hurt when I touch here."

"No."

"What about here?"

"No."

"It's blue so it must hurt a little."

"It'll be good as new by the game next week."

"Have you been icing it?"

"Sometimes."

"Sometimes?"

"Once."

"Once? You know better."

"Been too busy."

"Really? Doing what?"

"Wooing a certain blonde chef and convincing her to sell her property to me."

"Sounds two-faced to me."

"Why does everybody think I'm two-faced?" Doctor Harrison opened his mouth. "Don't answer. Maybe I was but not anymore. I've turned a new leaf. I want her property, but I want her to come with it, too."

"How are both going?"

"They both need a lot more work."

"Sounds unusual for you. Especially the wooing."

"I'll get the property. Later rather than sooner but her. She's different. Special. I need my—moves—so to speak, to be right. She needs more wooing."

"Well, well, well. I'm intrigued. Sounds like a turning point for our star defenseman. He might be showing vulnerability." He removed the blood pressure cuff from his bag. "The ankle doesn't look like more than a bad bruise, but we'll get an x-ray done when we get back to Montreal. Remove your jacket. I want to take a blood pressure reading."

Marc didn't want to.

"The jacket, please."

Hesitantly, Marc removed the jacket.

Doctor's Harrison's eyes rounded. "What happened to your shirt? It's ripped in two." He wrapped the cuff around his arm and slid the stethoscope under it.

"Compliments of the blonde chef—with my approval, insistence actually."

Doctor Harrison laughed as he inserted the stethoscope in his ears. "This sounds serious." He pumped the monitor. "I never thought you'd be serious about any woman."

Marc thought about it. "Yeah, well, she surprised me." How he felt about her surprised him, too.

"I met three beautiful women out in the lobby. Which one is she?"

"None of them. She went cold on me when she heard the helicopter."

He unwrapped the cuff. "Went cold? Your blood pressure's normal."

"Sad at the thought of me leaving."

"Really?"

He scowled. "Don't know. She accused me of being here only for her property. I needed more time to make her think I wasn't, but you arrived."

Doctor Harrison returned the cuff to his bag, removed his otoscope, and flashed it in Marc's eyes. "Would another night make a difference with her?"

"You saw the condition of my shirt and it was the first night."

"Of course. What would she rip the second night?"

Marc thought about it. "My heart if she didn't want to see me again."

Doctor Harrison stopped everything. "You *are* serious about her. I don't think I've ever heard you mention your heart."

"Why does everyone—including my blonde chef— think I'm incapable of being serious about a woman— no, don't answer." He didn't want to hear about his supposed inflated ego or being too concerned about himself to care about others. He wouldn't have gotten to where he was without an ego or being concerned just about himself. "I am serious about her. But she only sees me as the bad guy who wants to buy her property and kick her out. She sees me as an inflated ego."

"You are."

"And one more night would fix that. I would have more time to stop her from thinking of me as her egocentric arch enemy and to think of me as her savior and suitor. Her humble savior and valiant suitor."

"Humble, valiant, and savior, too? Really?"

"Fine. The good guy, trying to be humble even though savior and valiant would indebt her to me for life."

"I'm sorry for ruining your plan but I'm only obeying the coach's orders. Follow the light." He moved the otoscope from one side to the other. "Any dizziness?"

"No."

"Headaches?"

"No."

"Nausea or vomiting?"

"No."

"Slurring?"

"No."

"Did you black out when you hit the air bag yesterday?"

"I don't think so."

"Don't think so, don't want to tell me, or don't remember?"

"I don't think so," he said with more anger than he wanted, surprising Doctor Harrison. "I'm sorry."

Doctor Harrison stepped away from the bed. "The truth, Marc."

Marc put on his jacket. "I may have blacked out for a split second, but my head did hit the airbag."

Doctor Harrison waited. "I need to know everything."

Marc pulled up his sock. "I felt groggy after the accident and today. I had to wear sunglasses when I went outside. I've had headaches."

"I figured something along those lines. You blacked out. You're having headaches. You're sensitive to the light. Your reactions are slow, too, and you're getting angry." Marc kept his eyes averted as Doctor Harrison sat on the same armchair Katrina had the night before. "You were ready to play next week, Marc but you've aggravated your concussion."

Marc fisted the duvet. "Fine, I've aggravated it. But the symptoms aren't as bad as last year. I'll go through concussion protocols, no lights, lots of rest, no distractions, not even a text or TV and I'll be ready to play next week or even the following week—I won't even think about the blonde chef. Complete abstinence. Like holy orders."

Doctor Harrison remained silent.

"Please tell me I'm ready to play soon. I can't stay away any longer. I was off for most of last season and for three weeks this season. I can't stay away. I need to play."

"Let me get you back to Montreal and run some tests and a CT scan. Then I'll be in a better position to see where you stand."

"I'm sure they'll prove negative and I'll be good to go next week."

Doctor Harrison leaned forward. "Marc, you know as well as I do. Last year your symptoms didn't show up until a few days after the hit. It might be the same case here, too."

"It's not." Marc jumped off the bed and a wave of nausea and dizziness made him stumble.

"That doesn't look good to me, Marc. I need to get you in the hospital now and run those tests."

Marc sat down on the edge of the bed and waited until the dizziness and nausea subsided. This could not be happening. A major concussion last year and now another on the heels of a minor one. He couldn't be off another season. It would be two seasons in a row. Flashes of never playing hockey again made him want to throw up. He had to play. He could *not* not play. "I'm just tired and nothing more. I didn't sleep well last night."

"If the blonde chef gave you two Tylenol threes, then you slept like an elephant—even with her ripping off your shirt and whatever went with it."

Marc rubbed his forehead. He had to play hockey again and soon. It was his whole life.

"I'm going to give you another of Tyler's Tylenols. It should help you in the helicopter, until we get you in the hospital."

Marc waited while Doctor Harrison took one of Tyler's pills and came back with a glass of water. He swallowed it but didn't move for a long time.

"Now you tell me the truth, Doctor Harrison. If," he didn't even want to say concussion. "If this isn't the same as last year's, how long do you think I'll be off?"

Doctor Harrison put his equipment in his bag. "There's no science here. It could be days, weeks, or months. I'll know better once I run the tests and you've rested for a couple days."

"But if it's another major concussion, what are my chances of playing this season?"

"If it's as serious as the one last year, I would say you will be off for the rest of the season."

Marc didn't know if the room spun or he did. He gripped the duvet again to settle himself. "And my chances to play next season?"

"You shouldn't look so far."

"I need the truth now, too. Hockey has been my life for as long as I can remember. It was supposed to be for a lot longer." If this concussion was as bad as the one last year and he couldn't get over it, his hockey career was as good as over. He would never achieve the points, goals, trophies, awards, years of active playing or respect—the legendary status he wanted since he first played the game. He'd be short on all counts. He would be a has-been. A failure.

He couldn't be a failure. He couldn't come back to King Court short of what he set out for himself. Short of what his father and brother and everyone else expected of him. He was supposed to be larger than life. He couldn't be anything less.

"Let's just wait and see. I'm not going to make any predictions." Doctor Harrison took out his cell and walked to the window. "I have to tell Jacques."

Marc moved to one of the wing chairs around the coffee table and fell into it. His briefcase sat open and the folder, containing the papers Katrina needed to sign stared back.

Who was he kidding? Once those papers were signed, Katrina would never see him again. He would be the one who had robbed her of her home, her livelihood, her history, and her future—even if it was all her doing. She tried to make the inn better, and he respected her for trying, but she failed. She needed to put her failure behind her and go on with her life.

But once he took what was hers away, would he have any chance? Would she want to be with him? Could she ever feel anything for him?

No. He didn't have a hope in hell of winning her over.

She was right. They were simply a moment, and their moment together was over.

He was damned if he lost his hockey career and the chance at millions in the same day. He was damned if he hoped to be with a woman who didn't want the same as he did, who didn't even believe he had a heart.

He grabbed the folder from his briefcase and rushed to the door.

"Where are you going?" Doctor Harrison asked.

"To get my life back."

Chapter Eighteen

Marc strode to the lobby where coffee and pastries were set out on the coffee table. Jakob, Tyler, Eric, Ingrid, Rebeka, and Annelise sat around it, chatting and laughing with the helicopter pilot.

"Where's Katrina?"

The demand in his tone made them flinch.

"The kitchen," Annelise said, hesitantly.

Marc flung open the kitchen door, startling Katrina, who was pouring water from a kettle into a teapot.

"Everything okay?" She returned the kettle to the stove.

"Nothing is okay."

She moved to the counter and put the top on the teapot. "You didn't pass your physical?"

"Not in the least."

She frowned. "What does it mean?"

"It means my hockey career may be over."

"You can't be serious?"

"Does it look like I'm laughing?"

She picked up the teapot. "The crash made your concussion worse?"

"Unfortunately, it did. We just won't know how serious until more tests are done."

She put the teapot on a tray, averting her eyes. "I caused it."

"You didn't cause it. I swerved to avoid hitting

you. I'm not a monster, who has to pin blame on everyone except himself."

She balked. "I never said you were." She sighed, possibly to settle herself. "But once the symptoms are cleared, you'll play hockey again."

He propped his hands on the counter and leaned forward. "I may never play hockey again if it is as serious as the one I suffered last year."

She held the tray in mid-air. "Marc, you—"

"I shouldn't what? Are you going to sing platitudes like everyone else with wait and see and hope and pray?"

"I don't sing platitudes." She came around the counter with the tray and saw the folder in his hand.

Marc put the folder on the table and flipped it open to reveal the contract. "I need you to sign now, Katrina."

The tray jostled in her hands. "I thought you were doing a financial evaluation first."

"Let me give you a financial evaluation right now. A golf course will cost at least five million dollars and need another million or so every year to maintain. A water park with slides will cost anywhere between ten and twenty million, depending on the quantity and the size. And the figure doesn't include the necessary extras—like water, maintenance, health concerns, and so on. Tack on at least several more million each year for those things. Horse trails will run you at least one to two hundred thousand dollars per kilometer. As for cross-country trails and adapting hills for skiing, building in ski lifts, along with—"

Katrina slammed the tray on the counter, shaking the teapot. "Enough."

"But you wanted a financial analysis. Do you want to know how many people you need to attract here to pay back your loans and then how many more before you cut a profit?"

Katrina rushed behind the counter and kept her back to him.

"My best guess is ten to twenty years down the road to turn a profit." He tried to settle himself, but he was too agitated. "How am I or any of the other investors going to make any money now? We're in it for now. Not for the long-haul."

Her shoulders heaved up and down, but she didn't make a sound.

"Your proposal has no monetary value. Mine does. *Now* you can call me the bad guy for saying it like it is." A wave of dizziness made him sway. He pulled out a chair, sat down, and put his head between his hands until the dizziness subsidized. With it so did his emotions. "You have to let go, Katrina." It was a whisper. "You can't hold onto something that is dead and gone. It's ruining you. You had a good plan. You knew the inn could make money if you modernized but—"

She turned on him, her face red. "How do you know it was my plan?"

"Annelise let it slip. But it was sound. It could have worked if your parents thought so too. It just went—"

"Sour? Foul? Off the rails? I've heard more than my share of platitudes, so please spare me them, too."

He moved to the edge of the chair. "It doesn't mean you can't continue outside of the inn and restaurant. You can be so much more if only you let yourself."

"That's easy for you to say. Your plans didn't backfire on you and cost you your livelihood or the livelihood of your family or the people employed here. You don't lose anything. You have something out there, which may or not be in jeopardy, and soon you'll have everything here, which will be a sure-fire success. I go out with nothing except the label of the woman who made everything go to hell. I've got nothing except some scraps of paper in frames telling the world I was someone at one time."

He jumped up and grabbed her hands. "You tried, Katrina. Not everything we do will be a success. But you tried. It's more than most people can say. You should hold your head high."

"Hold my head high?" She all but spat out the words. "Tell it to my parents who lose everything and the people who lost their jobs."

"You and your parents and those other people will survive. You're burying yourself in the past, in what was and could have been but isn't. You have a future. You shouldn't be afraid to move on. We could even have a future together, but you don't believe in the sincerity of my feelings. You don't even believe I have any."

She threw off his hands and moved farther down the counter. "I know how you feel."

"No, you don't. I could have demanded you sign and been done with it—and you. But I didn't. I love you, Katrina." The words surprised him as much as her. But they were the truth. He loved her and saying it brought both a sense of satisfaction and excitement. But there was sadness, too. It wasn't returned. "Now you know how I feel." His voice was a whisper.

Katrina seemed grounded to the floor, her eyes glazed with fear. She looked like she wanted to run. "You can't."

"Why? Because it's only been twenty-four hours? Or you don't trust yourself to feel anymore? Or maybe you think I have such an overblown ego I'm incapable of loving anyone except myself? What is it? The question you should ask yourself is how do you feel about me? Do you think you could love me if you allowed yourself? Do you love me now? I feel a lot from you, but all I hear is we're just a moment. Are we just a moment or are you afraid of what you could be with me?"

Katrina looked away.

He waited, hoping she would give him a sign of hope but nothing. She didn't even seem to breath.

"Katrina?" He couldn't give up. She had to say something. She had to tell him how she felt.

But nothing. Absolutely nothing. She couldn't look at him. She even turned her back on him.

All hope faded. In one day—one hour—he lost his dreams and his heart. He couldn't lose anything else. He couldn't lose his spirit.

"You've come in loud and clear. You always do. Whether you say something or not." He moved to the table. "Now let me come in loud and clear. Sign now or I retract my offer."

Katrina swung around, gasping.

"Unless you can come up with another buyer in a week or two, you'll go bankrupt and lose everything. Keep calling me the bad guy, call me a bully, I don't care. This is all business now. Nothing but business. Just as you say it is."

"You can't mean it?" Her voice broke.

"You don't believe me now, either?" He pulled a pen from his jacket pocket and banged it on the papers. "Believe it. If you want to salvage as much as you can, you better sign now."

"I have to get my lawyer to look the papers over."

"They're the same as the ones I submitted to you earlier this week. Nothing has changed. Just sign them and let's get it over. The Acadia Inn and Acadia Restaurant had their day. You've had your day with them and it didn't work. It's my day now."

Her face went from red to white. He hated himself. He didn't want to see her in pain, but she forced his hand. He was what she believed. A heartless businessman with only the property and multi-millions on his mind.

"I need Ingrid to check." Her voice was just above a murmur. "She's read it. She can tell me if it's the same."

"Fine." He rushed to door. "Ingrid, can I see you please?" Ingrid came into the kitchen. "Could you please take a look at the contract? Katrina doesn't believe it's the same as the one I sent earlier this week."

Ingrid looked from him to Katrina and back to him. She sensed something was wrong. "Now?"

The question was asked to her sister, but he answered. "Now. I'm retracting my offer if Katrina doesn't sign now."

Ingrid's eyes rounded. "Katrina?"

Katrina moved to the table, holding her head high. "It's fine." She pulled out a chair and sat down but she was stiff. "Please make sure it's the same as the last one we all read, including Olivia."

Ingrid sat down beside her, pulled the folder forward, and looked it over.

Marc moved to the counter and rested his back against it even though he wasn't in the least composed. He wasn't sure if he was more angry than ashamed for his cold tactics or angry and ashamed at Katrina for thinking the worst of him. But the deed had to be done. The inn was a lost cause, and so was he with Katrina. It was her decision. He only confirmed what she refused. He didn't have to play nice anymore. He could be whatever he wanted. She wanted nothing of him.

Ingrid slid the folder to Katrina. "It's the same as the last one." She turned to face him. "You'll need a witness. Someone who doesn't have any vested interest in the inn. I'll see if Doctor Harrison can sign." She moved to the door and called him. Doctor Harrison came in, holding a cup of coffee.

"Doctor Harrison, this is my sister, Katrina," Ingrid said. "She and Marc need to sign these papers and we need you as a witness. It will sell the inn and property to Marc and his group."

Doctor Harrison's smile faded as his gaze went from Marc to Katrina. "You're all right with signing, Katrina? You too, Marc?"

Marc nodded as Katrina pulled out a chair for him. "I'm fine."

Doctor Harrison sat down while Marc sat on his other side.

Ingrid moved behind them. "Katrina, you sign wherever you see an x. Marc will sign the places with the check marks and Doctor Harrison will sign as the witness."

Katrina began signing, paper after paper, passing

them down to Marc for his signature, who then passed them to Doctor Harrison. When all the papers were signed, Ingrid gave a copy to Katrina and put a copy in the folder and handed it to Marc. "Congratulations, Marc."

Marc took it, placed it on the table, and covered it up with his hands. He wanted to cover up his face, too. But he shouldn't feel any shame. Katrina didn't leave him an alternative.

Doctor Harrison put his hand over Katrina's and squeezed. "I'm sorry. It wasn't a very nice way to meet you."

Katrina shrugged. "I hope you've had some pastries."

"The French macarons are the best I've ever had." He got up. "I'll be out there if you need me again."

Once he left, Marc stood up, holding the folder with both his hands. He couldn't look at Katrina and addressed Ingrid. "It will take at least a month if not more to process everything. The money should be transferred to the inn's account shortly after. My lawyer will inform your lawyer. I think the end of May was the agreed upon closing date."

Katrina stood up and handed the papers to Ingrid. "Can you scan and send them to Olivia and Amir? I'll let Mom and Dad know."

"Sure thing." Ingrid took the folder and disappeared into the hallway of the family's quarters.

Katrina moved behind her chair and turned to Marc. He wanted to look away, but he held his ground. He shouldn't be ashamed. It was all business. "We'll be out by the end of May as agreed." She put out her hand. "All the best. You got what you came for."

183

Marc couldn't take her hand. "It's not the way I wanted it to happen."

When Katrina realized he wouldn't shake, she pulled her hand away. "Neither did I."

Marc watched her walk toward the family quarters and disappear into a room. He did get what he came for.

So why did he feel he was leaving with nothing?

Chapter Nineteen

Marc stormed out of the kitchen and into the lobby, startling everyone. "Get ready to leave," he told Jakob, Eric, and Tyler.

Jakob jumped up. "Leave? Now?"

"Now."

In his room, Marc threw the folder with the signed contract in his briefcase and grabbed his coat from the armoire. He had everything he set out to get. He had the signed contract, selling him the inn and the property. Back home, the rough blueprints and projected earnings for the housing development waited for his approval. A tentative start date for demolishing the inn and for building the first phase of the massive community was even scheduled. Estimated demolishing time: July. Estimated building time: September. Once he put up billboards announcing phase one, King Court Development would be flooded with phone calls and emails inquiring about the townhouses and single-family homes. They would have the entire first phase sold by the end of the year. Families could move in by summer the following year.

He could see it all and was pumped to get everything rolling.

He still had his hockey career, too. He was the captain of the team that should make the playoffs, was an all-star every year since he was a rookie and won several Norris Trophies for best defenseman in the league. He earned himself a Hart Memorial Trophy for most valuable player and won both the Calder Memorial Trophy for best rookie and two Olympic gold medals. Along with one of the top salaries in the league, he had a lucrative sponsorship deal with a North American sports franchise store and a Canadian brewery. He lived the good life. Better than the good life. He had more money than any one man should possess and been with many of the most beautiful women in the world. No concussion or CT scan or team of doctors would decide when his hockey career was over. He was the master of his own life. He would play hockey again. If not sooner than he wanted, then a little later. But he would play again. It was a certainty as much as the development of his housing complex.

He had everything. He was enviable. He didn't care what people thought of him. Heartless or self-centered or cold. He had what he set out to get.

He would also make it into the Hockey Hall of Fame when he decided to retire. Once home, he would call his dad and tell him the news about the housing development. But his father would only tell him what he already knew. *I knew you'd do it, Marc.*

He would eventually tell his father about the possibility of another concussion, but the news could wait until it was confirmed by the tests.

Marc threw his coat on and grabbed his briefcase. He took a final glance around the room. At the bed he shared with Katrina. In the very place he now stood, he danced with her and sang for her. At the shower where he pulled her in against him.

He had everything and more.

So why the hell did it matter now what others thought of him? Why did he feel he had nothing?

The instant Katrina wished him success and left him standing all alone in the kitchen, all he had, all he had done, all he planned to do, all he was, blurred. It became nothing. Katrina meant everything to him and without her everything was insignificant.

This was not right. He'd get her out of his system. He'd get her out his heart. She was in his life a short twenty-four hours. It wouldn't take more than another twenty-four hours to get her out of his thoughts. His hockey career, his new business venture, his future success was forever.

Someone knocked on the door. He almost tore it off its hinges opening it. Eric and Tyler stood in the hall, looking both surprised and uncomfortable.

"Everything okay?" Tyler asked.

"Better than okay." He spied his gloves and toque on the night table. "Katrina signed and the inn and all the land we saw this afternoon belongs to us. Now get ready to make more money than you ever dreamed possible."

Neither Eric nor Tyler produced a victory smile. Their lack of enthusiasm wasn't right.

Marc moved to the night table. "I know you don't want to leave, you've had a great time." He stuffed his gloves and toque in his pockets. "But Jacques expects us back in Montreal for dinner."

"We're having a heck of time tearing Jakob away from Annelise," Tyler said. "He doesn't want to leave her."

"There are a lot of things we don't want to do but have to." His words made him sound cold. He was far from cold hearted. Maybe before it sounded right coming from him, but not anymore. But Tyler and Eric didn't know what happened. No one in the world knew what came over him. Nobody except him and Katrina, and she didn't believe him.

"I'll get my coat and start prying," Tyler mumbled and hurried down the hall.

Eric came into the room. "How did you get Katrina to sign?"

"Like I said, there are a lot of things we don't want to do but have to. This was one thing she had to do."

"You okay?"

Marc buttoned his coat. "Nothing will be okay with me until I play hockey again. Now get your things." He brushed past him, out the door, and to the lobby. Voices came from the kitchen. He didn't want to go in there. He didn't want to face Katrina, but he followed Tyler and Eric. Jakob was putting on his coat as Annelise, Rebeka, and Ingrid watched. Katrina, however, wasn't there. As much as he didn't want to see her, he wanted to. He didn't know when he'd see her again. If ever. He shivered. How could he believe another short twenty-four hours would clear her from his thoughts and heart?

"We're leaving now?" Jakob asked Marc. "Can't we finish our coffee first?"

"Tell it to Doctor Harrison. Where is he?"

"Heading to the helicopter," Tyler replied. Ingrid handed him his coat. "Is Katrina around?"

"She's talking to Olivia, our lawyer." Ingrid's gaze moved to Marc. "She asked me to say goodbye."

"Tell her thank you and we'll miss her cooking," Tyler said.

Ingrid nodded and gave him a hug. She grabbed

her coat. "I'll walk you to your ride." Tyler hugged both Rebeka and Annelise and went outside with Ingrid.

"Comic Con?" Eric asked, zipping up his coat.

Rebeka flung her coat on. "You're on."

Eric hugged Annelise and went outside with Rebeka. Marc saw all four moving toward the helicopter. Their dark coats reflected in the snow. He closed his eyes. He needed to wear his sunglasses and pulled them from his pocket. Thank goodness for the heavy-duty Tylenols. He would not manage the helicopter without them. Hell, he didn't think he would have managed Katrina without them.

"I guess the scones didn't work?" Annelise asked.

Marc pulled on his gloves. "Will you take care of her?" He couldn't. She wanted none of him.

Annelise threw her arms around him, startling him. "I will. I'm keeping in touch with Jakob."

"Anything you or your family needs. Anything Katrina needs—"

"I'll let you know. Even if it's behind her back."

"Even if there isn't anything to say, just let me know if she and your family are all right."

"Will do." She moved against Jakob, throwing her arms around his chest as he slung his arm around her shoulders. "It's not your fault you and Katrina didn't work out the way you wanted. I guess it was all business."

"It wasn't all business for Katrina. I robbed her of her livelihood." And her pride. He didn't know what was worse.

"Or maybe you gave it back to her."

"You're too young to be philosophical." He

softened. "It wasn't all business for me, either."

"Katrina will recover and open up some three-star restaurant somewhere in this wide world and call you to make scones for her."

Marc's smile was wry. "I'll hold onto the thought."

The helicopter pilot poked his head around the kitchen door. "Ready?"

Marc moved to the door and held it open for Jakob. He and Annelise couldn't say goodbye. Jakob finally pried himself away and rushed past him.

Annelise moved to the window and watched him go. Marc saw tears in her eyes and wished he and Katrina had the same innocence of first love. Then she'd be at the window with tears in her eyes because he was leaving, and he'd be making plans when next to see her.

Chapter Twenty

Katrina waited until she heard the helicopter leave. When she couldn't hear it anymore, she took out her cell and called her mother.

"Hello, Katrina. Everything okay?"

How was she to answer? "Everything's fine. How's Dad?"

"Much better. He's still weak, but he's walking around."

"Can you put the phone on speaker, please?"

"Hello, Katrina," her father said.

"Glad to hear you're doing better."

"Are the roads cleared?" her mother asked.

"Not yet. I would suggest staying another night there."

"Your aunt already prepared a bed for me."

Katrina was silent.

"Is everything okay?" her mother asked.

Katrina took a deep breath. "I signed the papers." There was silence on the other end. "I sold the inn." She closed her eyes, bracing herself for their reactions.

"It had to be done, Katrina," her father said, his voice low but strong.

"You did nothing wrong," her mother added.

Tears jumped into her eyes. "Then why do I feel I did everything wrong?"

"Because it's all you've known since you were

born," her mother said. "You tried to make it better, but it couldn't be done. We all tried. It just didn't go our way."

"We also put the burden of selling on you," her father said. "And we're sorry we did."

"I didn't mind. Anything to help you and Mom."

"Was it King Court Development?"

"Yes. Their offer was the best." She didn't want to tell them it was the only one on the table and necessity prevailed or that Marc would take his offer off the table if she didn't sign. Otherwise, she would have held off longer.

She couldn't tell any of it to her parents. It was all part of her ego complex. Her damn pride and inability to let go of what she believed belonged to her.

Funny though. The ultimatum upset Marc more than her. She needed the ultimatum. Otherwise, she would take the inn to the very brink of bankruptcy and disaster.

She was a fool. A selfish fool. She let things go too far and held onto, as Marc said, a dead vision. She was ashamed of herself. She put her wants in front of her family's needs.

How could she do that? She wanted to cover her face with her hands.

"Their offer was exceptional," her mother said. "The deed is done and now we move on."

"Once we've licked our wounds, we'll be fine," her father said.

"I think I've done enough of that already. I don't want to anymore." Even though she knew she would. One very unexpected wound, larger than the inn, restaurant, and property. The loss of Marc.

"I'll be home tomorrow, and we'll get things rolling," her mother said.

"I'm not an invalid," her father said. "I'll help out, too."

Katrina laughed as she wiped tears away. "You can handle the light duties, Dad."

"Like making you and your mother tea and adding the biscuit on the side?"

"It's always been your job. You know exactly how we like it." Katrina waited for her parents to say something more, but neither of them did.

"Everything will be okay," her father said.

Katrina nodded and was glad they couldn't see her. "I'll see you soon." She hung up before she cried again. They didn't need her tears on their conscience.

She could hear her sisters in their rooms. She didn't want to face them right now. They'd ask questions about Marc and she didn't have any answers.

She left her bedroom and went into the kitchen. It was dark outside, but the snow shed light inside. She flicked on the light and walked to her usual spot. The ranges.

The pots and pans used to make the *tourtières* were clean, but they sat on the counter. Next to them were the coffee cups, plates, and cutlery along with the leftover pastries. Her sisters brought them in from the lobby. Cleaning them was beyond their job descriptions. But at least they showed some compassion for her.

Katrina was about to wash them but decided against it. It didn't matter anymore, and she didn't have the energy. She was tired. Exhausted actually. It was as if everything she had gone through since they first put the inn and property for sale landed with a heavy thud on her shoulders. She didn't know what to do or feel. She should feel something but didn't know what. The loss of the inn? The loss of the restaurant? The loss of Marc? Or all of them?

She spied the scones Marc made on the opposite end of the counter.

The inn and the restaurant were losses, but Marc shouldn't be. She hadn't invested any emotion in him. She had refused to dream about him and about them together. He was a moment and nothing more. The inn and restaurant were her whole life.

So why did losing him weigh heavier on her mind and twist more at her heart than the inn and restaurant?

Marc loved her. Did she love him? He left her with the question before she turned and walked away.

Tears welled up in her eyes, making the kitchen a blur.

She moved to the table and sat down.

Yes, she did love him. She wouldn't be hurting if she didn't. She wouldn't be longing to see him and to ask for his forgiveness. Or to have him shield her from the ice and snow and tell her to believe in hope and a successful future. She wouldn't be crying if she didn't love him. She loved him but pushed him away. She had acted colder than he.

She wished she had broken down and told him the truth. She wanted him to stay with her. The inn and restaurant were beyond hope. He could take them from her and did. But instead, she used whatever little strength remained, to tell him nothing. To keep her head high, put the loss of the inn and restaurant in front of her as a shield, and say nothing. To use the loss as the excuse not to be with him or to think about her future.

She was ashamed of herself. Right now, she hated herself.

But it was probably better this way. It didn't matter if he loved her or she loved him. There were no ties this way, no emotions, and no hope between them. She accused Marc of an inflated ego, but she had a bigger one. She held onto a dead dream. She wanted to save her restaurant and the inn for her sake while playing with her parents' health and the family's financial well-being.

She didn't deserve Marc's love. She'd make a mess of love—of him, too.

She brushed her tears with her sleeve. She couldn't do this to herself. Allow her emotions to take over. How would anything get done if she did?

She looked around the kitchen. She knew every cup, corner, creaky tile, shelf and what went on it, but everything looked distant and obscure. She had observed her mother cook here and after graduating from culinary school, she rearranged the kitchen to suit herself. Just a few hours before, it was her home and refuge. Now it was unfamiliar. It felt like it didn't belong to her and come the end of May it wouldn't.

It was early January. She had until the end of May to sell everything in the inn and outside and move out.

If this was grieving over lost love, then she didn't have time for it. She had work to do. Not the kind to maintain the inn or property but to dismantle them. She would make herself a nice cup of tea, and if she was up to it, begin the process of selling everything. When her parents returned, they would find everything under control. They would see her resilience. She would have restored some of her pride.

An auction was the best thing to do. Everything was valuable in the inn. The hand-painted Meissen dinnerware. The pine and walnut furniture. The cherry wood and mahogany beds. The antique knickknacks and the one-of-a kind paintings. A good auction house would sell everything for her. Her accountant mentioned one. She'd ask for the name again.

Her parents had planned on taking an early retirement and moving to Florida before her father got sick. Once all the creditors were paid off, their retirement would take precedence. She would help her parents find a nice place in Orlando or Fort Myers or wherever they wanted to settle. Her father needed to rest in the heat of the sun away from any stress and her mother deserved to take care of herself, too. She was the original chef for the inn before Katrina and worked hard while raising her and her sisters. The last six months had made her mother weary and anxious. She needed to get strong again, too.

Her sisters would be okay. Ingrid practiced law in Toronto and Rebeka taught in Ottawa. They paid some expenses at the inn. Katrina noted everything and would make sure they got all their money back along with their share of the sell. They could then move into nicer apartments or buy condos. They deserved it, too.

Annelise was in residence at the University of Ottawa. She could stay there during the school months and then either move in with her parents or one of her sisters. She wouldn't graduate for another four years. By then, she would have a place, too, or Annelise could decide who to live with. In Florida with her parents. In

Toronto with Ingrid. In Ottawa with Rebeka. Or with her. Wherever she was.

Katrina held onto the table, needing support to hold herself up. When did she ever need support? This was all new to her—and frightening. It showed weakness. Weak she wasn't. Until Marc opened her heart. He made her weak. She had to close it up again. It was the only way to be strong. If she could. Could she?

She shook her head and the question away. But another question sprang up. Where would she be? Once the creditors were taken care of, her father's brothers given their share, her parents settled, and her sisters given their shares, she didn't think she'd have any money left for her. Served her right for making such a mess of everything.

On wobbly legs, she moved to the swinging kitchen doors and into the restaurant.

The room was dark except for the snow, shedding light through the window. The restaurant was exactly as she left it over a month ago securely locked behind closed doors. The Hepplewhite, shield-back dining room chairs with needlepoint seats and tables, the nineteenth century brass chandeliers with candles, the rich paisley balloon curtains, the handmade carpets.

This was all her doing. She brought everything together to suit her cuisine and create the right ambience.

But it was all for nothing. Just days before the reviewers arrived to assign it stars, she closed the restaurant and resorted to the cuisine customers wanted.

Now she had to sell everything.

She ambled to the bar and pulled out a stool. Several paintings by Marie-Anne Couture stared back at her. They were her favorites. A female servant in a long skirt, cooking at a fireplace in what was once the original kitchen of the Acadia Inn. Another was of a servant, an indigenous woman, holding a basket and picking herbs from one of the gardens in the back of the inn. The last was of a woman in her twenties, wearing a bonnet, staring back at her. It was a self-portrait of Marie-Anne Couture, who came to the inn as a young woman with nothing but a desire to work hard. Her great-grandmother taught her how to read and write. She took her under her wing and Marie-Anne never left. She painted by mixing her own colors from the food and plants around her and as an expression of herself and her thankfulness. She had no family except for her great-grandmother and the other people who worked at the inn.

Katrina sat taller. If a young woman of the late nineteenth century could leave whatever place she called home without any education, money, or support, she, a woman of the twenty-first century with all the support in the world, could do it, too.

She'd be okay. She was strong. It was an attribute as much as a weakness. She'd use her strength to move on with her life. Heck, she had an ego. She'd pull it out when it stopped licking its wounds and use it to get on.

She'd even manage without Marc. Her heart would heal, and she would forget about him. She had done without him before he literally collided into her life and upset it for those short twenty-four hours.

She put her head in her hands. If only she knew how she managed without Marc before he burst into her life for those brief hours. Then she could get off the stool and start there again.

Chapter Twenty-One

Marc couldn't stop staring at the inn. It was bare. Completely and utterly bare. Simply a shell of what he remembered. The hand-crafted wooden doors, shutters, and frames were gone, including the windows. He could see inside, and it didn't hold anything either. Even the veranda was stripped of the railing and woodwork. A plank replaced the steps, leading from the walkway to what once held thick double doors.

When he was here last in January, the entire grounds as well as the inn and barns were covered in snow and ice. Now the trees were budding. A few flowers were out too, but they were limp. They needed water but there was no one here to give them some.

The inn was deserted, and it had only been several weeks since it officially and legally become his, and Katrina and her family moved out. The inn and the grounds were nothing like that short time in January.

Marc ambled along the walkway, up the plank, and over the threshold into the lobby. It was mid-June, but the lobby felt colder than those brutal days in January. All the furniture was gone, including everything attached to the walls and the bar as well as the fireplace he cleaned. The hardwood floor was stripped to reveal cement. None of it mattered anymore. Soon bulldozers and wrecking balls would roll in and demolish the skeleton of what was once the over one-hundred-fifty-year-old Acadia Inn.

He lived up to his word. He sent Katrina a detailed financial analysis of the Acadia Inn, outlining all the services and perks she envisioned. It painted a sorrowful picture, exactly as he told her. There wouldn't be any monetary gains until ten years down the road. The housing development would earn immediate profits for the investors.

He sent her the analysis about a month after buying the property. It was now four months later. He expected to hear something, even a formal and trite acknowledgement from her lawyer. But nothing. Katrina didn't want anything to do with him. It was loud and clear. Just as it was five months ago in January.

"Whoa." Eric walked into the lobby. "It's only the frame in here."

Tyler stopped at the door and refused to enter. "It looks and feel like some old and abandoned spooky house from horror movies."

Jakob pushed him in. "It was all worth a fortune. Annelise said they got a lot of money for everything— more than they imagined."

Marc was glad everything brought in a significant amount of money. He knew how much the family was in debt. He also hoped once the creditors were paid off, and her family was settled, there was enough left over to get Katrina started, too. Wherever it would be.

Last he heard she was in Clearwater, Florida with her parents, scouting out condos. He didn't know if she thought of moving there, too. He knew she had looked for chef jobs at some restaurants but hadn't taken one yet. Annelise offered the information, and he listened, impartially even though his heart ached to hear more. He would have demanded to hear everything if Katrina inquired about him. He would even have raced to her and apologized profusely for bullying her and making her sign if she had. Then he would have dropped to his knees and begged for forgiveness.

The once grand and egocentric Marc Johansen was no more. Katrina stripped him to the bones and showed him what was more important than himself. He now wanted to prove how humble and contrite he was. If only she felt something for him. But she didn't.

Marc moved through the lobby and down the hall. All the doors, individually-carved pieces of woodwork, were removed. He peered into the guest bedrooms but there was nothing. Other than the walls and electrical wires hanging from the openings where light fixtures once were, there was simply an echo of abandonment. The handcrafted wood paneling was also gone, along with the safes built into the walls. Birds' nests were in the corners of the window sills and he wouldn't be surprised to see the homes of raccoons or squirrels in some of the rooms.

He moved to the bedroom he stayed in. Katrina and he danced in here, got soaked from the shower in the bathroom, and made love during the coldest night of the year. Yet he was warmer that night than any other.

A glint caught his eye from the corner. It was the turnkey to his room. He picked it up. Katrina hated it. She had trouble opening the door with it.

He grimaced, recalling her frustration. It was now a keepsake of the night. It was also symbolic. It was opening the door to the next part of his life. His life as a housing developer. As a magnate. But also, as a very overworked and bewildered housing developer. There was so much to learn and to see to about the business. The legal issues, the city development and planning issues, the architects and surveyors, the construction crews, the apprenticeships, and so on and so on. This was not hockey. He knew the game and how to coach and manage a hockey club. But he knew nothing about developing housing and learned on his feet.

He slipped the turnkey into his pocket. Unfortunately, it was also symbolic of a closure. It was time to close the door to his time with Katrina. He hadn't heard from her and stopped jumping to answer his cell every time it rang in the hope it was her.

Voices came from the lobby. He expected a full crew today. City planning officials, the architectural firm designing the first phase of the housing development, several contractors, and a real estate firm he thought of hiring to sell the homes.

He went back to the lobby but only the architectural firm had arrived. They carried laptops and tubes holding the various designs for the first phase of development. Once greetings and introductions were made, the head architect, a burly man in his sixties, ushered them into the kitchen where a makeshift table was set up.

Marc stopped at the threshold. What was once Katrina's sanctuary was now a barren room. Everything was gone, including the cupboards, wood cabinets, sinks, appliances, and countertops. The only thing standing was a large piece of plywood on logs, which acted as the architects' makeshift table.

As laptops were set up and blueprints spread out, Marc ambled to the pantry. Only empty shelves remained.

"Marc, you've seen the designs before but I'm going to explain them to Eric, Tyler, and Jakob," the head architect said. "I'll see the other investors later this week and go over the plans with them then."

"Go ahead."

Eric, Tyler, and Jakob gathered around the laptop and oohs and aahs were expressed along with lots of questions.

"Incredible," Jakob said. "So many houses and it's only phase one."

"Townhouses," the architect said. "I did, however, think about building bigger homes here, on this ravine, deeper into the property. It could be part of phase four. Marc, what do you think?"

With his hands in his pant pockets, Marc moved to the big hole once known as the kitchen window. "Will people who can afford a bigger home want to live in a densely populated community?"

"We can test it out," the architect said. "If someone expresses interest, then we can consider it." He explained everything to Eric, Jakob, and Tyler, but Marc closed them out. One of the barn doors stood open but there was nothing inside. The snow blade was gone and so was the tractor. The stable was bare, too. His high school buddy, Kyle, of Hewett Equestrian, had bought Macaroon, Principessa, Mistress Snow, and Rosiebelli. They would be used as draft horses to pull carts or carriages and for leisure rides.

On top of the inn and restaurant, Katrina lost Macaroon. But if he knew her well, she cut herself off from feeling that loss. It was the only way for her to push ahead. Marc couldn't blame her. Except it pushed him out, too.

He couldn't see the doors to Wilhelm Sherrer's wood-working barn and the barn where Katrina built a kitchen, but he assumed they were also empty.

Marc felt a tug of sadness and remorse. The community lost a valuable community program to rehabilitate at-risk youths. And Katrina and Wilhelm Sherrer lost another sense of self.

He spied the long branches and rocks the guys and Katrina's sisters used on that wintry January day to play hockey on the makeshift ice rink. They rested under the window of the stable, exactly where they left them. He could still hear them laughing as they body checked each other and scored.

His own father built ice rinks in the back yard of their home every winter. There he played hockey with his older brother who always outdid him. But he was glad his brother did. It made him play harder and smarter. Now his brother was a cardiologist in New York City with a beautiful wife who practiced family medicine and three energetic boys, and he was the hockey player. His brother's insistence on playing hard made him one of the best hockey players in the league. He glanced over his shoulder. Now he was also a housing developer or becoming one. If he knew what was involved instead of just dreaming about the money, he would have thought twice about forming King Court Development. He would have simply invested in the development like his hockey buddies. Not try to run the show.

Banging and voices came from behind the inn. Was someone there? Possibly Katrina?

Marc hurried out, his heart racing with the hope of

seeing Katrina. He stopped in his tracks. It was Lowan. He was putting wood of all shapes, sizes, and lengths in the back of a pickup truck. Several young men helped him.

Lowan pulled off his work gloves and extended his hand. "Marc, nice seeing you again. How are you?"

Marc shook it. "I'm good. I wasn't expecting to see anyone here."

"I hope you don't mind. I tried to get here before the closing last month, but I was tied up with some last-minute shoots. Wilhelm donated the equipment in his woodworking barn and whatever scraps of wood were lying around to the reserve. We're storing everything until we know where to put it. We've made several trips today, but this should be our last load."

"Take your time." Marc moved to the barn, which was supposed to house the kitchen. The doors stood open, but it was bare. Just like everything else. "Did you take the equipment in the kitchen, too?"

"No, there wasn't much except for counters and cabinets. Katrina donated them to the reserve. They're going to see who gets what."

Marc made one simple nod and walked back. "I was told the Sherrers employed a lot of people from the reserve."

"They only hired from the reserve. It was a big blow when the inn went under. But once the community knows who your project managers are, they'll make sure to get qualified people to apply for jobs."

"I'll put in a good word for them."

"It would be great."

The young men stopped loading wood. They gathered around Lowan and stared at Marc. None of them looked out of their teens yet.

"I believe they recognize you," Lowan said. "You can open your mouths and ask for his autograph, guys."

"How about selfies?" the tallest one with a pock-marked face of acne asked.

Marc not only took selfies with all three boys but signed autographs on pieces of wood or their caps.

"I was told you do a lot of work on the reserve," Marc said, watching the boys load several handheld saws into the pickup.

Lowan rearranged them. "I started off by recommending youth to Wilhelm's carpentry program, but my schedule became hectic and unpredictable and I got others to help. They took it one step further and expanded into apprenticeships by partnering with local colleges."

"What kind of apprenticeships?"

"All kinds. Wilhelm was involved with the carpentry program and Katrina wanted to start a cooking one, but they set up apprenticeships in electrical, plumbing, and bricklaying. Once they know who the companies are on the housing development, I'm sure they'll be in touch."

Marc felt the stirrings of excitement. The housing development would have community value after all. They could hire from the reserve and surrounding areas and open it up to apprentices. It sounded like a win-win operation. For him and the other investors and the community.

"I wish I could tell you who they are or when things will start but I can't." He indicated the people inside. "Too many officials involved. Lawyers, architects, politicians, you name it. I'm learning as I go along. Sometimes I think I'm improvising."

Lowan laughed. "I'm sure it's a far cry from hockey."

Marc nodded. "A much different world." A much different beast he wanted to say. "I'll give you the heads up once I know."

"I'd appreciate it. The team didn't go too far in the play-offs."

"No, we had too many injuries from key players and none of us were able to get back into the kind of form to go deep into the play-offs."

"You were sorely missed."

"I came back for our final month, but I was only allowed a certain number of playing minutes. I'll be back in top-notch form next season and playing what I should."

"Good to hear. How will you manage hockey and," he indicated the kitchen where everyone hovered over the laptops and blueprints, "developing houses?"

Marc sighed. "Good question. Don't have an answer right now. Hockey is still going to be number one, but I don't want to stretch myself thin. You seem to manage a robust acting career and helping out on the reserve when you can."

"Acting brings in the money and gives me an above average lifestyle. It certainly doesn't hurt my social life, either. I live a good life, but I couldn't live without this part of my life, too. Everybody knows who I am here, but it doesn't matter. Sometimes I'm just Lowan, the half-First Nations and half-Scottish guy, whose father happens to be an RCMP official and sometimes I'm Captain Borgman, who saves galaxies and people. It doesn't matter to me who people think I am. What matters is relating to the kids here. I could have been an at-risk youth if I didn't have chances and support. Seeing a kid go from feeling he or she is a nobody with nothing to feeling he or she is a somebody with something is as rewarding as an acting job. It's just becoming harder and harder to get here. I'm stretched thin, too. I'd like to say I hate getting new roles, but I don't."

"It's a nice problem to have."

"I'm trying to find others to help out, but role models for these kids isn't as easy as you would think. I've been mentoring these three lugs for years now. All of them are headed to university next year."

Marc watched the boys organizing the equipment in the back of the truck. They were laughing as they jostled each other.

He couldn't believe what he was about to say but he wanted to say it and wholeheartedly. "Would hockey players be any good as role models?"

"Hockey players would make better role models than an actor playing the role of a half-man, half-cyborg captain."

"Then sign me up. And I think I can go one step further. I work with a lot of guys, who can move beyond their nice lifestyles and their egos and give a little of themselves, too. I'll see if I can get some mentoring program started with the hockey league. I'm sure female hockey players would be interested, too."

"Whatever you can do to help would be great." Lowan took his hand in both of his and shook it enthusiastically. "I know the Sherrers and the others who worked on the reserve wouldn't agree right now, but the housing development will be good for the community. It will create lots of jobs and opportunities."

Marc pulled up his shoulders and raised his head high. Finally, some good. "I'm glad to hear. It means everything coming from someone who lives here and has attachments to the inn."

Lowan indicated the inn. "You're being hailed." Eric stood at the window, motioning him in. He waved at Lowan, gave him some odd salute, which Lowan mimicked, and returned to the others at the makeshift table.

"It was good talking to you, Lowan. I'll be in touch." He moved back inside. Everyone invited to the meeting had arrived and was listening to the architect speak about the project.

Marc was glad he could employ tradespeople from the reserve and excited to hear it was welcomed. But he couldn't stop thinking about being a mentor and possibly starting a mentorship program with the hockey club. The front office brass always wanted him and the other players to do community work. He would suggest the mentoring program and see what they did. The housing development ensured jobs and apprenticeships for the community. It ensured economic growth, but it could have social value, too.

Good was coming out of the housing development. If it wasn't for Lowan and those three young men, he would not believe it.

So why wasn't he happy? Why didn't he have the same enthusiasm and drive for the development as he did for hockey? Why didn't he even have the same as Eric, Tyler, and Jakob, who asked question after question and got more and more excited? This was supposed to be his future after hockey. Why wasn't he as thrilled about the venture as he was before his Range Rover plowed into a wall and an angel rescued him? Why did it not matter anymore how much money he made and what others thought of him?

Chapter Twenty-Two

Katrina's heart raced wildly. In just five short minutes she would open the doors to her very own restaurant.

The Acadia Bistro was at the corner of a cobblestone road on the edges of Old City Montreal. It was prime real estate, but who would ever believe the paintings of Marie-Anne Couture could be so valuable? Not even in her wildest dreams could Katrina imagine getting so much money for a previously unknown nineteenth century female painter. The paintings, twenty-five in all, were bought by a private collector, who set them up in his little art gallery in Toronto. They brought in more money than the family got for everything else in the inn.

Katrina sold all of them except for her three favorite ones, which had hung in the Acadia Restaurant. All three now were displayed behind the bar of the Acadia Bistro.

She kept the paintings in lieu of money, which could have come her way. She wanted them as a reminder of one of the Acadia Inn's success stories. They also reminded her of herself. Working hard and surviving, but not without ups and downs and losses, of the past she lost and still grieved for, and also of her future and its promise of hope and joy. They were a reminder to dream and believe again.

After paying creditors and sharing the remainder of the money with her uncles, sisters, and parents, Katrina could afford the hefty down payment on the property, which included the restaurant, an enclosed outdoor patio, and a second-floor apartment. The property was owned by one of her former culinary teachers, who retired to focus on writing cookbooks and spending time with her grandchildren. When she suggested Katrina take it over and refashion it to her taste, she was hesitant. But after some deliberation she became excited at the prospect of giving her cuisine another try.

Since the only chef jobs to come her way were too junior or inappropriate for her style of cooking, the decision was reached quickly. Now it was up to the restaurant's success to continue the payments and give her peace of mind—and up to her to keep the restaurant a sound business success. She failed big-time with the Acadia Inn and Restaurant. She didn't want to experience that kind of loss again. But she was realistic and honest this time. Her pride didn't cloud her judgement. She took another chance. As Marc said, she was a risk-taker and she was proud. It was how she should be. No more beating herself up. No more talk of failing or failures. No more talk of pride as a negative attribute when it made her strong again. This was what she had to do. It was in her, and she was happy to do it.

She just hoped and prayed and hoped and prayed some more that this venture didn't blow up in her face, too. How many risks could she live through and survive?

She wondered what Marc would think of her turnaround.

No, she had to get Marc out of her mind, unless he

forgave her and came to the opening in the evening. She wanted to see him but even more, she wanted to thank him. He'd sent the financial analysis of her ill-conceived dream for the Acadia Inn and property, which now lay in the drawer of the buffet in the bistro. She didn't read it, but she wanted to acknowledge it just the same. He was a man of his word. He was honest. He helped to set her straight.

Her father ambled up beside her, wearing a snappy dark blue suit and lively red tie. The heart problems took a toll on him. He was always a lanky man, but he was thinner now and appeared to have aged beyond his sixty years. He was, however, doing better. The trauma of the demise of the Acadia Inn was a done deal, and he was at peace and getting stronger. He played golf with close friends again, which he hadn't done since the demise of the inn.

He put his arm around her shoulders. "Two more minutes to go, Katrina."

"I'm so nervous."

"It will be a wild success. You were hidden away at the inn basting ribs when you should have been out here, creating the menu you always wanted. You know you're better."

She kissed his cheek. "You have to say it. You're my father."

"True, but when have I ever told you anything you cooked was nothing less than spectacular?"

Katrina thought about it. "When I was five and made you the chocolate cake in my Easy Bake Oven."

Her father laughed. "It tasted like plastic. But I still ate it."

Katrina's hair brushed against her bare shoulders as

she shook her head. "I don't know how you did."

"Since then everything has been wonderful."

Her mother came out of the kitchen. "Are you sure I can't help in there? I'd love to try my hand at the wild boar stew with the incredible collection of mushrooms."

Katrina took her arm. Her mother looked like her old self again. She dyed her hair to her natural blonde coloring, mainly out of all her daughters' insistence, and walked, swam, and read books again. She was as much at peace as her father and Katrina had to admit, as she was, or soon would be, if the restaurant was a success. If this venture didn't bomb on her.

No. Positive thinking only. It wouldn't bomb.

"Tonight, you're my guest, Mom. No cooking for you." She fixed the collar of her mother's royal blue dress. "And if anything goes wrong, my support."

Her parents lived with Rebeka in Ottawa after they left the inn but now stayed with Katrina in the apartment over the restaurant even though it was far from arranged. Other than a bed and a sofa, nothing else was set up. Katrina still lived out of suitcases. She emptied all her luggage and boxes to find the little black dress and sling-back heels she wanted to wear for the opening. Finding jewelry to match entailed another hunt.

Katrina smoothed down the dress. She'd prepared the menu and wanted to cook but was the hostess tonight. She hired a friend from culinary school whom she admired, a couple sous chefs, including Lowan's youngest sister, Megan, and three servers. For now, she was the pastry chef. All the sweets were prepared. Her father was all set to act as sommelier if the need arose or to step in as host while her mother was more than ready to help out in the kitchen. The reservations' list on her iPad told her she was booked solid tonight until closing and for the next two weeks, but she was still frightened.

Her cell buzzed. Katrina checked her phone. It was five o'clock.

Her mother squeezed her hand, a big smile on face. "Time to open the door to your new future."

"You're too sentimental, Mom."

"It's what moms are for."

"Drum roll, please," her father said.

Shaking her head, Katrina unlocked the door and stepped out. A mid-September wind shifted her clapboard. She straightened it and arranged some flowers in the urn at the door of the outdoor patio.

"Tally ho."

Eric, Tyler, and Jakob, looking polished in suits and her sisters all decked out in dresses and full make up, approached the Acadia Bistro.

"Tally ho isn't what I was thinking." Katrina kissed them all on the cheeks. "Welcome, welcome, welcome."

"You have legs," Tyler said. "I didn't even recognize you."

"Have to look the part of the hostess—even though I'd rather hide in the kitchen."

"Not tonight, Ms. Restaurateur," Eric said. "Tonight, it's all about you."

"Are we the first guests?" Jakob asked, holding Annelise's hand.

"You are." She held the door open for them. "And the champagne is ready for my first guests."

As they went inside, Katrina looked up and down

the road. People were moving about, other restaurants opened, too, but she didn't see the man she hoped she would.

She'd extended an invitation to Eric, Tyler, and Jakob and, with her heart in her mouth, called Marc. His voice mail kicked in, but she extended an invitation—and ended with a stupid, "let bygones be bygones" platitude. He must have loved it—if he even bothered to listen to the message. But she didn't hear from him. Even Jakob didn't know if he would come. He spoke to Marc, but he didn't mention the message or the invitation. As far as he knew Marc was still visiting his brother in New York.

Katrina closed the door. It served her right. She pushed him out of her life in January and now he did the same to her. Marc had moved on. She was happy for him. It was all she wanted for him. To be happy. Playing hockey or developing his plans for the housing community on the inn's property. Whatever. She just wanted him to be happy.

But she hoped he would come. If only to make amends for being so nasty about signing and hurting him. Let bygones be bygones and all that inane stuff. But he had better things to do with his time than to come to the opening of her restaurant. He probably moved on to some other woman, too.

She hated the thought of another woman but didn't have time to wallow in self-pity. From the instant Eric, Tyler, Jakob, and her sisters walked in, toasted the success of the bistro and drank their champagne, Katrina was swept off her feet with guest after guest and dish after dish. Even her parents who she hoped wouldn't work pitched in with the guests on the patio or wine recommendations or clearing tables. Everyone raved about the food and said they would come back.

It was almost midnight when Katrina put the mop away and closed the lights of the restaurant. She was dead tired. She kicked off her heels after her last guests and cleaned up. The chefs left the kitchen spotless and the servers did their part in the dining area, but Katrina said she would clean the floor and get the tables ready for the next day. She would open for lunch tomorrow and needed everything in order before she climbed the one set of stairs to the second floor and fell onto her sofa. Her parents went up about an hour ago and were probably fast asleep in her bed.

But she had one more thing to do. Marc didn't come. It was time to break all ties to the past—and to him.

She opened the drawer of the buffet and took out the envelope containing the financial analysis. It was time to dump it and be done with the Acadia Inn, the Acadia Restaurant, and Marc.

She heard scrapes coming from the patio. A table and chair were moved around. Someone was out there.

She put her heels on, grabbed the mop, and moved outside to the patio. A table and two chairs were set up and a person sat at it. All the other chairs and tables were removed from the patio and locked in the back. How had a table and the two chairs been forgotten? She placed the envelope on the hostess stand and was about to tell the person the restaurant was closed when her heart leaped. Tears sprang into her eyes. But they weren't tears of sorrow as they were in January. These were tears of joy. It was Marc. He came after all.

Marc held up a bottle. "Cognac?"

She laughed.

"Unless you're going to use the mop against me first."

Katrina placed the mop against the wall and ambled toward him. It was dark with only the lights from the streets and any of the other opened restaurants, but he looked at ease in a suit with his shirt opened at the collar. Her heart couldn't stop racing. It was as though she were seeing him for the first time. He was the most beautiful sight in the world.

"I didn't think you were coming," she said.

"I had to wait for the cognac to arrive."

"From where?" She pulled out the chair and sat opposite him.

"From some little duke's castle hidden away in Avignon in the south of France." He pulled out a snifter from one jacket pocket and a second one from the other.

Katrina laughed. "You brought the snifters, too?"

"I wanted to be prepared." He poured some cognac in each and held one out for her. "The cognac is worth about the same as the motorcycle parked on the other side of the road. You can understand why I only brought two snifters." He lifted his glass. "To the success of the Acadia Bistro. And to you."

"To success." Katrina took a sip. It was smoother than the one she remembered having with him in January, but it was older. It made her insides go warm. "It's wonderful."

Marc agreed. "I see you're still wearing just black."

"It's my downfall."

"Far from it. You look good. Healthy."

Katrina laughed. "Healthy?" Her aim was professionally sexy. "Well that's a word I've never been told I look like."

He took another sip, his gaze always on her. "You look good in that smile, too."

Katrina shuffled in the chair. "It's been a long time since I've had something to smile about. You look healthy."

"Never felt better. Just have to stay healthy. Training camp starts next week and the season in a month."

"No more problems with the concussion?"

"As of April, I've been symptom-free."

She twirled the liquid around. "You made the play-offs."

"I thought you didn't care for hockey?"

"It was on the news. And both Annelise and my dad told me."

"Did you watch any games?"

Katrina didn't want to tell him she hadn't. She couldn't bear the thought of seeing him and remembering she pushed him out of her life. She shook her head. "Too busy."

"I can believe it. We did make it to the play-offs, but we didn't go far. This year will be better. We're all in top form and strong and eager to go again."

She took another sip. "I heard the inn and the barns were torn down and development is starting soon."

"It is." He looked into the liquid for a long time. "I've handed King Court Development over to a management firm."

"A lot of work?"

"Too much of it." He put the snifter down but kept

his hand around the stem. "I sold it."

Katrina sat up. "What?"

"I haven't told anyone yet, except for my family. But I am keeping my investment in the housing development."

"I thought it was supposed to be your retirement."

"It was but it took over my life. It's been nothing but an aggravation of the kind I don't need and want. It was a challenge when I was buying the property and inn but the minute I did it turned into a nightmare. Eric, Tyler, and Jakob aren't losing sleep over their investment. Neither are the other backers. They're enthusiastic and eager. Thoughts about it don't keep them away from hockey either. But I'm losing sleep and it's keeping me from hockey. Hockey is my life. I was a fool to think I could manage the company and the development of the housing complex and play hockey at the same time. I can't. Developing the property for housing is way above my skill set and knowledge. I just want to play hockey. I want to play until I can't contribute any longer. Even if it's cut short, which I'm hoping it's not. Then maybe I'll try my hand at coaching or managing. I don't want the worries attached to King Court Development."

"I'd like to say I'm sorry it didn't work out, but I don't think you're sorry."

"No. I'm relieved. Very relieved. I can go back to what I really want without any worries and give it another run. If I can't play, then so be it."

"It's quite a turnaround from the last time we spoke."

"Yes, I made an about face. I'm hoping there's going to be more to me than just recognition as a hockey player."

"You're not just any hockey player."

"No, but I didn't want to push the inflated ego business." His smile was wry but sexy as always. He took a sip of his cognac. "I've…" He took a longer sip. "Well, I…"

Was he at a loss for words? Katrina couldn't believe it, but he was. "Is something wrong?"

"No, not at all. It's all good. I've, well, I've taken a page from you and your father's books. I've set up a temporary woodworking site and a kitchen for at-risk youths on the edge of the property."

Katrina put her snifter down. Did she hear him say what she did? He wasn't the altruistic type. "You have?"

"It's only in a temporary location right now. But, yes, I have."

She laughed. "Temporary or not, I think it's wonderful. The need is there, Marc. The youth will benefit from it."

"I'm glad to hear it. I was, well, I was hoping your dad could put in some time with the woodworking workshop, get it started, so to speak, and train a few volunteers." He gulped down the rest of his cognac. "I was also hoping you could help out with the kitchen program if you had time. It needs to be set up."

Katrina leaned forward. "What happened to the almighty Marc Johansen?"

Marc's laugh was shy as much as it was sly. "He learned humility. He learned there's more to the world than just him and hockey and money."

Katrina moved back against the chair. She wanted to cry. "I would be honored to help out. But only if you do me a favor first."

"Anything."

She got up, took the envelope from the hostess stand, returned to the table, and slid it toward him. "Only if you burn this or throw it in the garbage, or play hockey with it, first."

Marc picked it up. "It's the financial analysis I sent you." He turned it over. "You didn't open it."

She shook her head. "I didn't need to." She grimaced. "The Acadia Inn is finished. The Acadia Restaurant is finished. They're in the past. I'm looking ahead now. I took another risk. Well, actually two risks. I set up the bistro and," her voice went lower, "I called you." She cleared the emotions from her throat. "I'm sorry if I didn't believe you the last time we spoke. My, well, my heart believed but my head and my pride wouldn't. Thank you. For everything."

Marc spied the trash in front of the patio. He got up, threw it in a bin, and returned. He poured more cognac in both snifters. "To the future and moving on."

"To the future." She took another sip. "But you've done more than set up the carpentry and cooking program. Lowan was here and said the hockey club started a mentorship program on the reserve. You, Eric, Tyler, and Jakob are the first mentors and several female hockey players are involved, too."

"I can't take the credit for the program. I put the bug in the front office brass' ears and they arranged it. They brought it to the attention of the league and a lot of my other hockey buddies will volunteer with other reserves and communities across Canada and the United States."

"It's still wonderful news. It doesn't matter who

takes the credit."

"This is where you can say something about my inflated ego doing good beyond myself."

"My apologies but *my* inflated ego was stroked too many times tonight, so I can't think beyond mine right now. But it is wonderful."

Marc laughed. "Good turnout?"

"We're booked solid for the next month."

"Congratulations."

"Thank you." They sipped in silence for a while. "We're closed, but I could make you something to eat."

"Another time."

Katrina put her snifter down. "I'm," she had to tell him. "I'm glad you came."

"You invited me. I believe your actual words were to let "bygones be bygones". I wouldn't have come if you hadn't extended the invitation."

She looked long into the cognac, then raised her gaze to Marc. He was waiting. Intently. Expectantly. "I might have said a little lie."

"A little lie? Really, from you who always told it as it is?"

"I wanted you to come, but I also wanted to tell you I was sorry."

Marc leaned forward and rested his arms on the table. "More sorries? I should be the one apologizing for arm-wrestling you into signing."

"I needed to be arm-wrestled. No, I wanted to apologize for me. For how I ended," she paused and then spilled it. "For how I ended us. I wasn't truthful."

Marc moved his chair closer and put his elbows on the table. His gaze mellowed into hers. "You want to be truthful now?"

"Will you allow me? Will you allow me to answer your question now? The question you asked me, and I couldn't or wouldn't answer? Or is it too late for the answer?"

Marc waited. He held his breath. "You'd better be prepared to tell me you love me, or I've just spent thousands of dollars on a bottle of cognac to impress and romance the hell out of you."

Katrina laughed and clasped her hands over his. "No need to impress or romance the hell out of me. There's no need to do anything. I can't tell you how often I thought about it. About you." She pulled herself closer. "I love you, Marc." Tears filled her eyes. Tears of joy for finally telling him, tears of sorrow for not telling him before, and tears of regret for what she had done. "I knew I loved you then, but I just couldn't say it. Pride or ego or fear, I have no idea what it was that held me back. I still love you. I love you, now."

Marc was beside her, pulling her up. "Katrina, my greatest fear the last few months has been you." He cupped her face. "I love you. And I want you in my life, permanently and forever."

"I've had too much happiness today, Marc."

"You can never have enough happy in any day."

"Are you two going to ever kiss?" came her father's voice from the upstairs window.

Katrina jumped out of Marc's arms even though he held onto her. She was appalled. "Dad, have you been listening?"

"No, but your mother has."

"I have not!" came her mother's voice.

"You know I like the window open and you're my daughter. I was listening in case I had to come down and protect you. And I'd be happy to help out with the woodworking program."

"Hello, Mr. and Mrs. Sherrer," Marc said with a laugh. "And thank you."

"I assume you're the man who Katrina has refused to talk about," her father said.

"She has no choice but to talk about me now. I'll even come up, introduce myself, and confirm honorable intentions if you'd like. No need for you to come down and protect her."

"Are you going to bring up the bottle of cognac?"

Marc's eyebrows shot up. "I'll make sure and grab two extra snifters on our way up."

"We're in our pajamas, Wilhelm," her mother said.

"We'll come down," her father said. "In respectable clothes. Bring him inside, Katrina."

"Not to worry, Dad, I will." Katrina slung her arm through Marc's and led him to the door of the restaurant. "I'm sorry. They're staying with me. I didn't think they'd eavesdrop."

"Not a problem. Do they know who I am?"

"You mean do they know you're the bad guy who bought the inn and property and the good guy I love?"

Marc's eyes rounded. "That pretty much sums it up."

"I have three sisters, Marc. They know everything and more but like good parents, they don't let on how much they know."

"So I won't be kicked out of the restaurant?"

"Not with a bottle of a rare cognac—and me holding onto your arm." She grabbed the knob, but the door was locked. "Uh-oh."

"Did the god of power outages tell the god of new

restaurants something?" Marc asked.

"Possibly."

"Well, since everything is going better than planned, I have something else for you." He pulled a brass object out of his pant pocket and placed it in her hand. It was the turnkey from the inn.

Katrina was surprised. "Where did you get it?"

"I found it on the floor of the inn."

"Should I consider this the key to a new beginning?"

"Yes, but with me. Think of it as a betrothal, to use one of Great Aunt Hazel's words." He slipped it on her finger. "Not the right size but we'll work on it."

Katrina removed it but held it in her hand. She wrapped her arms around his neck and gave him a long overdue kiss.

Marc, however, pulled her away. "Your parents are coming down. I don't want to give your father an excuse to use the mop on me."

"If they weren't, and I hadn't locked us out, I would have dragged you into the kitchen."

He turned her to face the city. "I want you to look over there at the tallest building."

"They're condos, aren't they?"

"I live on the eighteenth floor."

"You mean you've been so close all the time I've been here?"

"I've wanted to run over every hour of every day. I only came when I got your message."

Katrina kissed him again. "Did I tell you I love you?"

"You can always tell me. After you give me a private tour of your new place, introduce me to your parents, and we drink another cognac, we're going to tell them we're, how would Great Aunt Hazel put it?"

"Go dancing?"

"Sounds about right. We'll start with a waltz, a salsa and then a tango, throw in a cold shower, some wonderful singing, possibly even a little hockey and, of course, I will always let you score."

Katrina laughed. "We can't forget the scones."

"Definitely, scones. What would happen if I baked you a cake?"

"Would it have icing?"

"Oh, you don't want to go there."

"Oh, yes I do!"

A word about the author...

Under the pseudonym of Kirsten Paul, Franca Pelaccia has written two romantic comedies, *The Hockey Player and the Angel* and *The Detective and the Burglar*.

She has also written an action/adventure/mystery novel entitled *Moses & Mac*, the first book of the Vatican Archaeological Service series.

Writing as Francesca Pelaccia, Franca self-published *The Witch's Salvation*, a historical paranormal novel that won the Beck Valley Reviewers' Choice Award for 2013.

An avid reader, Franca reviews novels for the Historical Novels Society.

http://francapelaccia.com